JONATHAN .... north coast
of New Sou............ and far too
.... children. He was born in New Zealand and still

Also by Jonathan Harlen

The Cockroach War
Brain Scam
Circus Berzerkus

JONATHAN HARLEN

DROP DEAD, Mad Dog Fred

ALLEN&UNWIN

First published in 2003

Allen & Unwin
83 Alexander St
Crows Nest NSW 2065
Australia
Phone: (61 2) 8425 0100
Fax: (61 2) 9906 2218
Email: info@allenandunwin.com
Web: www.allenandunwin.com

National Library of Australia
Cataloguing-in-Publication entry:

Harlen, Jonathan, 1963– .
    Drop dead mad dog Fred.

    For children.
    ISBN 1 74114 169 9.

    1. Bank robberies – Juvenile fiction. 2. Fathers and
    daughters – Juvenile fiction. I. Title.

 · A823.3

Designed by Wayne Harris
Typeset in 12/18 pt Goudy by Midland Typesetters
Printed by McPherson's Printing Group

contents

the rescue

It was hot.

It was so hot that even the rocks had blisters.

It was so hot that a goanna sunbaking on a sand-hill had passed out, and was beginning to sizzle.

It was so hot that emu eggs were cracking open in their nests, and frying themselves.

Samantha Tucker had been riding her kangaroo all day along the dusty trail, looking for two wombats that had strayed from the herd. It was late afternoon and she was tired and saddle-sore. Her trusty farm kangaroo, Spring, was still hopping along gamely underneath her, but he wasn't happy. He badly needed a drink, which is why Sam took a detour off the trail to a nearby waterhole.

When she got closer, Sam saw that the waterhole

had dried out and turned to mud. She was just about to give up and head for home when she spotted something. It was a pair of ears. In front of these ears was a pair of eyes, and in front of those eyes was a snout, just barely showing above the surface of the waterhole.

The ears and eyes and snout belonged to a dingo, trapped in the mud.

The dingo was gradually sinking. It was well on its way to becoming a fossil. In another minute it would be completely covered in mud, which would do wonders for its complexion, but nothing for other vital organs like its heart and its lungs.

Tired and hot as she was, Sam couldn't just stand there and watch this dingo die. She had to do something. She dismounted, and took a long coil of rope out of her saddlebag.

'Hang on, dingo!' she called. 'Wait right there!'

The dingo had been waiting for quite a while. It had no plans to go anywhere. '*Rrrk!*' it said, trying to bark through the thick mud. '*Mmmf! Grrrb!*'

Sam took one end of the rope and tied it around Spring's hindquarters. Then she took the other end and waded out. By the time she reached the dingo, she was in over her knees. She took one more step and all of a sudden sank in up to her waist, so she was just as stuck as the dingo was.

2

'Darn,' she said.

'*Grrb?*' the dingo said. Its ears drooped a little. It looked at Sam anxiously.

'No worries,' Sam said. 'I've still got hold of the rope. Spring'll pull us out. She's the strongest kangaroo this side of the Black Stump. Either that, or we'll be dug out by a passing archaeologist in a couple of million years.'

She pushed the end of the rope down into the mud and underneath the dingo's stomach. She brought it up the other side, and, after a fair bit of mucking around, she tied the dingo up as neat as a Christmas present (a very *muddy* Christmas present, but let's not get too picky). Then she took hold of the rope with both hands and tugged it to get Spring's attention.

'On the count of three!' she called, wondering as she did so if kangaroos knew how to count. 'Give it everything you've got, boy! You're our only hope! One! Two! *Three!*'

Spring tensed the muscles in his powerful hind legs, and did exactly what his name suggested. He sprang. He yanked on the rope as hard as he could, and with a tremendous glurking, glooping noise, Sam and the dingo shot free of the mud. They skimmed over the surface of the waterhole until they hit dry land, then bounced and skidded across the ground like a pair of demented waterskiers, while Spring bounded on ahead.

'Whoa, boy!' Sam yelled to him. 'That's – *ow!* – that's enough! Stop! Put on the bra-a-a-a-a-akes!'

Farm kangaroos are obedient creatures. Spring stopped at once, and waited patiently while Sam tried to untie the rope from around the dingo. This wasn't easy, considering how muddy and slippery the rope was, and how muddy and slippery the *dingo* was, after its pleasant little dip in the waterhole. It was a bit like trying to untie a bar of wet soap wrapped up in slime. But finally she got it done.

'There you go, dingo!' she said triumphantly. 'You're free as a bird.' Surveying the mud-coated animal in front of her, she added, 'And I tell you what, you sure could use a birdbath.'

That was when it happened – the strangest thing Sam had ever seen in her life.

The dingo stood up on its hind legs, folded its arms, and talked.

talking to a dingo

'You don't exactly look like a plate of lamingtons yourself,' the dingo said. 'Why don't you go find a mirror in that saddlebag of yours, and take a look?'

'I don't have a mirror,' Sam replied. 'I don't have a kitchen sink, either. It's a saddlebag, not a removal van.'

At that moment Sam realised what she was doing. She stepped back, eyes wide and pressed a hand to her forehead.

'I'm talking to a dingo,' she muttered. '*I'm talking to a dingo!*'

Sam always kept a Colt .45 twelve-gauge boomerang tucked into a holster on her belt, in case of emergencies. She whipped it out and aimed it right between the dingo's eyes.

'Look,' she said. 'Just because I rescued you and we went through a near-death experience together, it doesn't mean you have to start acting all weird. Why don't you cut the crazy stuff and bark a couple of times, or maybe howl, like a nice normal dingo?'

The dingo grinned. It had the whitest, flashiest, toothiest smile Sam had ever seen. Any used-kangaroo salesman would be proud to have a smile like that.

'First you risk your life to rescue me, and then you pull out a boomerang and *shoot* me?' it said. 'I don't think so. I think you're bluffing. That boomerang probably isn't even loaded.'

'Stop talking!' Sam ordered. 'Dingoes aren't meant to talk. It's against the laws of nature!'

'Well, there you go,' the dingo said. 'That just shows how extraordinary I am. Not only am I devilishly handsome, and wickedly intelligent, and the best digger-upperer of emu bones in the business, but I can also talk the hind leg off a bandicoot. I'm one in a million. The pick of the bunch. The cream of the crop. You did yourself a huge favour, rescuing me.'

'I did?' Sam lowered her boomerang. 'How?'

'Well . . .' The dingo took a deep breath, but then choked on a blob of mud that dropped from its snout into its mouth. '*Gak!* Ugh, that tastes terrible! This mud is driving me nuts! You wouldn't have a towel in that saddlebag of yours, would you? I could really do with a rubdown.'

'Sure,' Sam said. 'It's right next to the mirror. In the ensuite, up the stairs, second on your left.'

'Okay, I get the picture,' said the dingo. It stepped to one side and gave itself an almighty shake. Mud flew off everywhere, in all directions. By the time the dingo had finished, it was spotlessly clean. Sam, however, was considerably dirtier.

'Ahhh, that's better,' the dingo said, smoothing down its fur with its paws and casting an eye over itself admiringly. 'Excellent. No need for a towel after all. Nothing like a good shake to get rid of a few unwanted kilos, and make you look trim, taut and terrific. Now, where was I?'

'You were telling me what a huge favour I've done myself,' Sam said, wiping a glob of mud off the end of her nose. 'I can hardly wait.'

'I'm glad to hear you're so excited,' the dingo said. 'Because it really is a *huge* favour. Bigger than you could possibly imagine. You may not believe this – in fact you probably won't – but where I come from, dingoes don't only talk. They perform miracles.'

'Do they?' Sam said, not believing a word of it. 'You don't say.'

'That's right, kid.' The dingo patted its chest proudly. 'I'm a genuine pure-bred *miraculous* talking dingo. One of the last of a dying breed.'

'Okay, I believe you,' Sam said, 'But one thing bothers me. If you're so miraculous, how come you didn't miracle yourself out of that mud back there? How come you needed me to come along and rescue you?'

'Ah.' The dingo grinned again. 'That's the catch. You see, we miraculous talking dingoes can only do miracles for *other* people. Not for ourselves. That's part of the brief.'

'The brief?' Sam said.

'The rules,' the dingo explained. 'The job description. We find poor, humble farming folk such as yourself, struggling to make a living on the harsh, unforgiving plains of the Outfield, and we offer them a miracle. Maybe we offer them beans to grow a giant beanstalk. Or a goose that lays a golden egg. Maybe we offer them a porridge pot that's always running over with porridge. Doesn't that sound wonderful?'

'It sounds dumb,' Sam said. 'Now if you'll excuse me, I've got to get going.'

'*Dumb!?*' The dingo looked flabbergasted. 'What's the matter with you? This is the chance of a lifetime, and you're telling me it's *dumb?*'

'I'm not interested,' Sam said. 'I'm glad I rescued you, and I've enjoyed our little chat, but I don't want a beanstalk, or a goose that lays golden eggs, or an overflowing porridge pot, or anything else. I'm perfectly happy just the way I am. And right now I really need to leave, because I've got to get home by sundown, so I can milk the wombats.'

She coiled up the rope and began walking with it back towards Spring. The dingo looked puzzled for a moment, then trotted along beside her.

'You *milk* wombats?' it said. 'I thought you ate them. Not that I'd know anything about that, of course,' it added hastily. 'I'm a *vegetarian* pure-bred miraculous talking dingo, myself. Can't *stand* the taste of wombats. Nasty, horrible things.'

'We milk the heifers, then churn the milk to make cheese and butter,' Sam said. 'We make the best Hairy-Nose cheese and butter in the Outfield. That's how we make our living.'

'Are you sure you don't want a miracle?' the dingo asked. 'Turn your wombats into alpacas? Make them produce strawberry-flavoured milk?'

'Thanks but no thanks.' Sam finished packing away the rope and swung herself up into Spring's saddle. 'We don't need anything. And you'd better not come nosing around our farm, because my father's not too fond of dingoes. He skins them and turns them into fluffy dingo-skin slippers.'

The dingo shrugged. 'Suit yourself,' it said. 'You can't say I didn't try. But look, if you ever change your mind——'

'I won't.'

'But if you ever *do*, at least let me tell you how you can find me. I live deep in the desert, at a place called Malagar. Ever heard of it?'

Sam frowned. The name certainly rang a bell somewhere in her mind, but she couldn't remember where she'd heard it. 'Maybe,' she said.

'It's a hidden paradise of rainforests and underground caves and crystal-clear mountain streams,' the dingo said. 'You follow the setting sun westward, until you find the Sacred Tree. Then you stand in the shadow of the Tree when shadows die, and the Secret Door will open.'

'What?' Sam frowned. 'Stand in the shadow of the tree when shadows die? That's impossible!'

'Not impossible at all,' the dingo replied stiffly. 'I've been doing it for years. Twice a day and three times on Sundays. Haven't stuffed up once.'

'And how far am I supposed to follow the setting sun into the desert?' Sam asked. 'A hundred kilohops? Two hundred? Five?'

'Until you find the Sacred Tree, I told you that,' the dingo said impatiently. 'Come on, kid. You have to do *some* of the work yourself.'

The mention of the word 'work' reminded Sam. She really needed to get going. It was a long way home, and her parents would be cross if she wasn't back in time for the milking.

'Well, anyway, nice talking to you,' she said. 'I'd better get a move on. Don't go getting stuck in any more waterholes.'

'I won't,' the dingo said. 'And just remember, Samantha Tucker, when things go from bad to worse, when your world's falling apart, and you're at your wit's end, and you're thinking "Only a miracle can save us now", that's the time to come to Malagar. I'll be waiting for you.'

'Thanks.' Sam looked puzzled. 'But how did you know my name? I didn't tell it to you, did I?'

The dingo grinned mysteriously. 'Maybe you did, and maybe you didn't,' it said. 'Could be a lucky guess. Or it could be . . . a miracle.'

With those words it dropped down onto four legs and bounded away, in the direction of the desert. Sam watched it go, then with a quick tug on Spring's reins she turned and hopped off down the trail.

wombat stew

Sam didn't waste any time thinking about the dingo on the way home. She was too busy thinking about the chores she hadn't got done, because she'd been out all day searching for the wombats.

Sam was twelve. She'd been working full-time on her family's wombat farm since she was eight. Every day she had to check the herd, fix the fences, take out the hay, do the milking, chop the wood, feed the kangaroos, weed the garden, churn the butter, sharpen the knives, plait the ropes, peel the vegetables, and muck out the stables.

And that was just before breakfast.

Mostly, at the end of each long day, she was so plumb tuckered out she couldn't even make it to her bed. She simply opened the door of her bedroom, staggered forward a few paces, then fell with a crash, face-first onto the floor.

Life on her family's wombat farm had always been tough, but in recent months it had become almost impossible. This was partly due to the drought, and the wombat rustlers, and an outbreak of Mad Wombat Disease that had killed a quarter of the herd. But there was another reason as well. Another even more terrible disaster had hit the Tucker family.

An accident had happened to Sam's older brother Billy.

Billy was fifteen. Before his accident he was the best roo-boy Sam had ever seen. There was nothing he couldn't do once he got into the saddle. He competed in roo-deos all over the Outfield, and tamed the wildest bucking broncaroos. He mustered wombats like a seasoned pro, and rode up and down slopes so steep they would frighten a rock wallaby.

Sam had never forgotten the day the accident happened. She and Billy were mustering wombats together up along Sunstroke Ridge. Billy spotted a small herd of red flyers, the biggest and wildest bucking broncaroos of all, and took off after them at once, calling for Sam to help him herd them into Deepfry Canyon, so the leader could be caught and brought home.

It was a mad, exciting chase. Eventually Billy lassooed the leader, then decided he wanted to ride it, right then and there. He leapt on it, bareback, and set off at a frenzied gallop across the narrow, winding canyon floor.

Riding any kangaroo bareback is dangerous, as you'll know if you've been to kangaroo-riding lessons. Riding a wild bucking broncaroo bareback through a narrow, winding canyon is just about the craziest thing any roo-boy or roo-girl can do, short of throwing their boomerangs blindfolded, then trying to catch them with their teeth.

The broncaroo bucked Billy so hard and so far that he looked as though he was flying. He tumbled through the air and landed horribly, banging his head against a rock.

When Sam reached him, a thin trickle of blood was coming from his mouth. She thought he was dead. Then, as she stroked his hair and pleaded for him to be all right, he opened his eyes and smiled at her. But when he tried to get up, he couldn't move.

He couldn't move *anything*.

He was paralysed from the neck down.

It was an hour after sunset when Sam finally got home. Smoke was curling up from the chimney of the homestead just up ahead of her, and lights were shining from the windows. As she hopped up the path past the milking shed and the stables, she caught the beautiful smell of dinner wafting invitingly down the hill towards her, on the cool evening breeze.

Mmmmm, she thought, sniffing the air deeply. *Wombat stroganoff*.

She dismounted and led Spring to his trough. She tethered him and rubbed him down, then went inside.

'Hi Mum, I'm home!' she said, as she wandered into the kitchen. 'Sorry I'm late. I couldn't find those two wombats anywhere.'

'Never mind, I'm sure they'll come home by themselves eventually,' her mother Alice said. 'I'm just about to dish up. You hungry?'

'You bet.' Sam plonked down in one of the chairs and watched as Alice ladled huge spoonfuls of wombat stroganoff onto three plates. Her mouth began to water as the rich, spicy smell of the stew filled the room. Sam had always liked womburgers, and wombat rissoles, and wombat-tail soup, and wombat *a l'orange*, but wombat stroganoff was definitely her favourite.

'Mum,' she said. 'Have you ever heard of a place called Malagar?'

Alice stopped and stared at her. 'Malagar?' she repeated. 'Yes, that's a name from a story I used to tell you when you were little. An old Aboriginal legend.'

So that's it, Sam thought. *I knew I'd heard the word before.*

'Tell me the story again,' she said. 'I've forgotten it.'

'Well . . .' Alice hesitated. 'I don't remember all of it. I haven't thought about it for years. It was a story about a great Aboriginal warrior who found an oasis in the desert: a magnificent lost paradise, full of palm trees and waterfalls and underground caves, and surrounded by high bush-covered hills. When he got there he made friends with a dingo that could talk. The two of them went to find the Great Dingo, who was the leader of the talking dingo tribe, and the Great Dingo granted the warrior a miracle.'

Sam felt her throat go suddenly dry. Her heart was thumping in her chest, and the palms of her hands were sweaty.

'A miracle,' she repeated, trying to keep her voice as normal as possible. 'That sounds interesting.'

'He had to pass the ultimate test first, though,' Alice went on. 'It's a very difficult test that hardly anyone ever passes.'

'But he did pass it?' Sam asked. 'The Great Dingo did grant him his miracle?'

'Oh yes. There was a great famine in the land, and the warrior asked for food for his tribe. That very day, according to the legend, the sky began raining bandicoots and wallabies, and the tribe was saved.'

Sam's head was spinning. She'd begun to wonder if she'd imagined the conversation with the dingo. It had been a scorching hot day, and she'd been tired and thirsty. Stranger things had happened, out there at the edge of the desert.

Suddenly she frowned. 'Where's Dad?' she asked her mother. 'How come you're only serving up three plates, not four?'

'Oh, he'll be in later,' Alice said. 'He was feeling a bit down about everything, you know how it is. The drought. The rustlers. The Mad Wombat Disease. Not to mention the stress of trying to run the farm without Billy.'

Sam nodded. She knew exactly how her father felt. The Tuckers had only just managed all the work on the farm when there were four able-bodied people, but now with only three – and with Alice having to stay home most of the time, to care for Billy – it was simply impossible to get everything done.

'D'you want me to take in Billy's dinner?' she asked. 'I'll sit and eat with him if you like.'

Alice nodded. 'He'd love that,' she said. 'He's been looking forward to hearing about your day.'

Sam picked up two plates of wombat stroganoff and walked down the hall to Billy's bedroom. Billy was lying on a big, comfortable bed, propped up by pillows. The room was in the shade of a large plum tree, so it wasn't too hot. Outside the open window, galahs and lorikeets were screeching and twittering in the branches.

Seeing Billy there, Sam fought off a feeling of desperate sadness. He had been lying like that, in the same bed, in the same room, every day since his accident. Every day Alice changed his pyjamas, and washed him, and shifted him a little so he wouldn't get bedsores. Thanks to this tender loving care, he still looked perfectly healthy: a strapping teenage boy with a freckled, open face and thick, curly dark hair. It was only when you got close to him that you could see that his arms and legs were thinner than usual; his muscles wasted from lack of use.

'Hey, Billy,' Sam said, as she set the two plates on a card table behind the bed and sat down. 'What's new?'

'Ah, y'know.' Billy grinned. 'The usual. Climbed

a mountain in the morning. Wrestled a croc in the afternoon. Regular day at the office.'

Sam smiled. Her feelings of sadness always disappeared once Billy started talking. He was always in such amazingly high spirits. He'd once told her that he'd never given up hope of making a recovery. Every morning when he woke up he opened his eyes and thought, *This is it. This is the day I'll be able to walk again.* It never happened, but believing it *might* happen was all that kept him going, he said.

'Listen, Sam.' Billy's face grew serious for a minute. 'We're in trouble. Dad's finally cracked. He went out to do the milking, then came back with a bucket on his head and said he was off to become a bushranger.'

'A *bushranger*!' Sam exclaimed. 'Oh no!'

'He said he couldn't stand by and watch his farm go down the drain, and see his wife and children starve,' Billy went on. 'He had to do something. So he's headed off to rob the bank at Backward Point.'

'*What?*' Sam leapt to her feet. 'But that's crazy! He doesn't know the first thing about robbing banks! He'll get caught for sure!'

'I told him that,' Billy said. 'But he wouldn't listen. His mind was already made up. "Say goodbye to plain old Fred Tucker!" he told me. "Say hello to Mad Dog

Fred the Human Feeding Frenzy, the Terror of the Outfield!"'

Sam groaned, and buried her head in her hands. 'No,' she said. 'He hasn't. Please tell me he hasn't.'

'He has,' Billy said.

'Not Mad Dog Fred the Human Feeding Frenzy!' Sam groaned again. 'Anything but that! And he's wearing a bucket on his head? A *milking* bucket?'

'Yep,' Billy said. 'It's pretty daggy. He looks like an upside-down mop.'

'This is a total disaster,' Sam muttered. 'He'll get caught and thrown in jail, and it'll just be me and Mum running the farm. This'll ruin us completely.'

'You never know,' Billy said. 'Maybe we should look on the bright side. Maybe he won't get caught. Maybe he'll rob lots of banks, and hold up lots of stagecoaches, and we'll all be rolling in money.'

'Get a grip, Billy,' Sam said. 'Dad can't even *spell* bushranger. He thinks a stagecoach is a person who teaches acting. He thinks highway robbery means stealing a road.'

Billy grinned. 'I know, I know. He's not the smartest person in the world. But he is our dad.'

Sam headed for the door. 'Look, he's a good, hard-working wombat farmer, and a great husband and father, but he'll never make a bushranger,' she said. 'We both know that. I've got to stop him, Billy. I've got to get out after him, right now, before anything terrible happens. Did he say where he was headed?'

'Not exactly,' Billy said. 'He just said he was going to rob the bank at Backward Point in the morning.'

'In the morning. Good. That means he'll be camping somewhere along the trail.' Sam hurried into the hall, and glanced at the clock opposite the hatstand. 'I can still catch him. Then all I've got to do is persuade him to come home.'

She returned to the bed and knelt down beside it. She patted Billy's arm, even though she knew he couldn't feel it, and looked into his eyes.

'Thanks, big brother,' she said. 'I wish you could come with me. It's not the same riding the range without you.'

'Stay away from those bucking broncaroos,' Billy said, and managed a lopsided smile. 'They're murder.'

Sam felt tears pricking at the corners of her eyes. She blinked them away fiercely. 'One day you'll be better,' she whispered to him. 'One day I'll *make* you better. I don't know how, but I will. And that's a promise.'

mad dog fred

4

As soon as Sam had finished dinner she prepared to leave. She re-saddled Spring, and re-packed her two saddlebags, putting in a compass, her bush-knife, her water-bottle, her lassoo, two Colt .45 twelve-gauge boomerangs, some dried food and cooking gear, and her sleeping blanket, rolled up tight.

Alice came out onto the front porch to see her off. 'Take care, take care!' she called out as Sam rode away. 'Don't get lost! Don't talk to strangers! Put on a fresh pair of underpants, every day!'

'I will!' Sam called back. 'Goodbye! Look after Billy! Goodbye!'

Sam knew the way to Backward Point backwards. She'd gone there with her parents many times, taking wagonloads of premium-quality Hairy-Nose butter and cheese to sell at the markets. Still, travelling was different at night, and it seemed ages before she reached the small junction town of Deep Gully, halfway to her destination.

From Deep Gully, roads led out across the plains to all the main towns of the Outfield – Long Off, Extra Cover, Square Leg, Wide Mid-On and Deep Midwicket. Sam took the road leading north to Backward Point. She followed it steadily for another two hours, until she came to a narrow, winding river. From here, Backward Point was only half an hour away. Sam could see the lights of the sleepy little farming town twinkling faintly in the distance. She continued along the river's edge for a short while, until, out of the corner of her eye, she spotted a column of grey smoke rising from behind some trees.

She led Spring towards the smoke. Sure enough, there was Fred Tucker, sitting on a log in front of a campfire, roasting a scrawny-looking goanna on a stick. Fred was a big man, with a plain, lumpy potato face and an unruly mop of flaming red hair. Several of his front teeth were missing, and a sizeable chunk had been knocked out of his left ear, where Frisky, his favourite farm kangaroo, had kicked him.

Frisky was at the campfire too. He was tethered to a nearby tree.

Sam leapt off Spring's back, and crashed through the last of the undergrowth to meet her father. 'Dad, Dad!' she called out. 'Dad, it's me, Sam!'

Fred got such a fright that he dropped his goanna into the fire. He picked up his wombat milking bucket, jammed it down over his head, and drew a Colt .45 twelve-gauge boomerang from his holster.

'Hmmt!' he shouted, from underneath the wombat bucket. 'Whmm Gmms Thmmr?'

'Dad, take that bucket off your head!' Sam shouted. 'It's me!'

'Hmmt!' Fred said again. 'Stmmp Mm Imm Shmmmt!'

'Dad, take that stupid bucket off your head!' Sam yelled as loudly as she could. 'It's me, Sam!'

Fred lowered his boomerang. He couldn't see a thing out of the wombat bucket, because it had no eyeholes. He couldn't talk properly because there was no hole for his mouth.

'Smm?' he said. 'Im Thmmmt Rmmmly Ymmm?'

'*Yes!*' Sam almost screamed.

Fred whipped the bucket off his head and tossed it to the ground.

'Well, blow me down!' he said. 'It *is* you! You're a sight for sore eyes! Come here and give your old dad a hug!'

Sam braced herself. Her father's hugs always left her feeling like a freshly squeezed orange. His arms were extremely muscly from years of shovelling wombat droppings out of the milking shed.

'That's it! Big hug! *Bi-i-i-ig* hug!' Fred picked her up and crushed her so hard she felt her ribs bend like palm leaves.

'So what are you doing here?' he said, after he had put her down again. 'Hang on a minute. You haven't come all this way looking for those two wombats, have you?'

'No, Dad,' Sam said, gasping for air and feeling her chest to make sure her ribs were all right. 'I've come to see you.'

She picked up her father's wombat milking bucket and looked at it in the light from the fire.

'You know, you really ought to cut some holes in this,' she said. 'That way you'll be able to see out.'

Fred took the bucket from her, and stared at it. A delighted smile spread slowly across his face.

'Cripes,' he said. '*That's* a good idea.'

'And another for your mouth,' Sam went on, 'so people can hear what you're saying.'

Fred gazed at his daughter admiringly. 'That's brilliant, Sam!' he said. 'Absolutely brilliant! I can see you know a bit about this bushranging lark.'

He sat down on the log in front of the fire, still staring at the bucket. He seemed to have forgotten completely about the half-roasted goanna he had dropped into the flames, which was now burnt to a crisp. After a few moments he looked up.

'I knew you'd come, Sam,' he said. 'I knew you'd join me. You couldn't stay home day after day, working yourself into the ground, watching our farm go to rack and ruin. You had to do something. You've come to be my backside-kicker, and follow me to riches and glory.'

Sam sat down on the log beside him. 'That's sidekick, Dad,' she said. 'Your sidekick. Not your backside-kicker.'

'Eh?' Fred frowned. 'Yeah, righto. You can be that too, if you like.'

'Actually, I haven't really come to *join* you.' Sam said, trying to break the news to him as gently as she could. 'I mean, not that there's anything *wrong* with being your backside-kicker, or your sidekick, but——'

'Damn right there isn't! Stick with me, kid, and I'll make you a legend!' Fred said. 'Together we'll be the most infamous bushrangers ever! We'll be infamouser than Captain Starlight! Infamouser than Captain Moonlight! Infamouser than Captain Midnight, and Captain Twilight, and Captain Toilet Light, and Captain Bedside Light, and all those other useless old dirtbags!'

'There never was a bushranger called Captain Bedside Light, Dad,' Sam said. 'Or Captain Toilet Light, either.'

'What are you talking about?' Fred leapt to his feet. 'Sure there were! Captain Toilet Light was the terror of the Outfield for years! And Captain Bedside Light – what a tragic story *that* was! Hung by the troopers for stealing a rusty piece of fencing wire from his own farm!'

'If he took it from his own farm,' Sam replied, 'how could that be stealing?'

'Exactly!' Fred said. 'It was a terrible injustice! He was an innocent man! There he was, about to be hung in the town square, in front of thousands of onlookers. All hope was lost. Suddenly he looked out at the crowd in front of him, pressed his hand to his heart, and uttered his famous last words – "Time for lights out now. Nighty-night." *That's* the kind of bushranger I'd like to be, Sam.'

'What, a dead one?' Sam said. 'Hung by the troopers for something you didn't do?'

'No, no!' Fred said. 'I won't be hung by the troopers! They'll never catch me! Especially not if *you're* with me, Sam. We'll outsmart them every time.'

Sam stood up. 'Dad, listen,' she said. 'You're a great wombat farmer, and the best dad Billy and I

could wish for, but the fact is you're just not very . . .
I mean, you don't have the . . . you can't be a bushranger, Dad. You'll end up dead, or in jail for the rest
of your life, and the farm'll be ruined. You've got to
give it up, right now.'

'Give it up?' Fred looked horrified. 'But I haven't
even started yet!'

'You don't have a criminal mind,' Sam said
desperately. 'You're too honest. You're too nice. You
don't think the way bushrangers do.'

'Aha!' Fred winked at her. 'That's what *you*
think! I've got a plan, Sam. I've drawn a master plan
of *exactly* how I'm going to rob the bank at Backward
Point tomorrow morning. Come and look.'

Reluctantly Sam followed her father around to
the other side of the campfire. There lying on the
ground was a stick – a plain, pointed stick with no
goanna roasting on the end of it. Next to this stick,
just visible in the flickering firelight, was a drawing
that Fred had made in the dirt.

It was a large, wobbly-looking square. Inside the
square, written in capital letters, was the word
BANK. On the left-hand side was written another
word: WINDOW. And along the side at the front
was written a third word: DOOR.

'It's all in the planning, Sam.' Fred gazed down

proudly at the drawing. 'Gets 'em every time. Now, can you tell me what this thing is here?'

He picked up his stick and tapped at a spot on the drawing. Sam looked closely.

'It's a stick,' she said.

'No no no,' Fred said. 'I mean what I'm *pointing* at with the stick.'

Sam looked closely again. 'Judging by the sign saying "DOOR", I'd say that's the door,' she said.

'Exactly.' Fred nodded. 'It *is* the door. And when we arrive, after we've tied up the kangaroos and I've put my wombat bucket on my head, we go in through that. You with me so far?'

'Uh-huh,' Sam said.

'Good. Tell me if it's getting too complicated. Now, what's this thing here?'

Sam looked again. 'The window,' she said.

'Exactly. That's the window. And when we arrive, after we've tied up the kangaroos and I've put my wombat bucket on my head, we *don't* go in through that.'

'We don't go in through the window,' Sam said. 'Okay.'

'Because if we do, we'll smash the glass and probably slice our noses off. My advice is to stay away from the window completely.'

'Stay away from the window,' Sam repeated. 'Right.'

'And the roof,' Fred went on. 'Stay away from the roof as well. If we get up on the roof, after we've done the robbery, we'll just have to get down again. There's nowhere to go except to another part of the roof. So we come out exactly the same way we go in.'

'Through the door,' Sam said.

'You've got it!' Fred slapped Sam heartily on the back, then wrapped his arm around her shoulder and gave her another crushing hug. 'I told you! You're a natural! It's not just one brilliant criminal mind we've got, Sam! It's three! No – two! With my brain and your prawn, this plan of mine is foolproof!'

'That's brawn, Dad. Brawn. Not prawn.'

'Sure it is! You see what I mean? With you around, those troopers don't stand a chance!'

Sam was lost for words. Fred took his stick and used it to fish out the *other* stick: the one with the charred remains of his goanna roasting on the end of it. He brought the goanna up close to his face and gave it a sniff.

'Dad,' Sam tried again. 'You don't have to do it like this. There's another way.'

'I know,' Fred said. 'I could fry it. But I didn't bring my frypan.'

'I meant you don't have to be a bushranger!' Sam said. 'You don't have to rob and steal from people to save the farm! It's wrong, Dad! It's against the law!'

Fred dusted a few glowing embers off the goanna, then bit off its head. 'I'm disappointed in you, Sam,' he said, as he munched. 'I thought you were on my side. I thought you were here to *help* me.'

'I *am* here to help you,' Sam said. 'I am, I just——'

'Then don't tell me to give up and go home!' Fred roared. He waved the goanna wildly and shouted, 'I've had enough! I've got to do something! Don't you understand? There's a time in every man's life when he's got to roll up his sleeves and get his hands dirty! If you've got a problem with that, if you don't want to watch me robbing banks, then go! You're either with me or against me, and now's the time to decide!'

Sam hesitated. She'd known her father was desperate, but she'd had no idea he was this bad. It would take time to make him change his mind. Meanwhile, she could either stay and try to keep him out of trouble, or go home and leave him at the mercy of the troopers.

'Don't worry, Dad,' she said finally. 'I'm with you all the way.'

hold-up at backward point

Next morning Sam woke with a cold, wet nose pressing against her cheek. She sat up with a start, and bumped her forehead against Spring's neck.

Spring was scratching at her shirt with his paw, making worried clicking sounds with his mouth.

'What is it, boy? What is it?' Sam rubbed her eyes and yawned. She noticed how high the sun was. It had already risen well above the horizon.

'I know it's late, but we're not on the farm today, Spring,' she said. 'We're robbing a bank. And bank robbers don't have to get up at dawn.'

She glanced across at her father, who was sprawled out on his blanket next to her, snoring loudly. 'Go and get him up too,' she said to Spring. 'Tell him it's time for breakfast.'

A short time later the two of them were sitting around the campfire. Sam prepared a hearty breakfast of leftover wombat stroganoff and damper bread, which she had brought with her in her saddlebag. Then it was time to go.

'Now remember,' Fred said, as they hit the open road. 'I'm the expert bushranger, and you're just the raw recruit. You're here to listen and to learn. Did you bring any boomerangs?'

'Two,' Sam said.

'Colt .45 twelve-gauges?'

'Of course.'

'Great. Take them with you into the bank. But remember, they're dangerous weapons. Don't throw them unless you have to.'

Sam nodded. Unlike her father – who couldn't hit a barn door if it dropped on him out of a tree – she was a crack shot with a boomerang. She could slice the wings off a mosquito at a hundred metres. On a dark night. In a raging cyclone. Unless she wanted to *kill* the mosquito, that is. Then she got it right between the eyes.

'And remember to be polite,' Fred went on. 'We're here to rob people, not to be rude to them. So we always say "Thank you" when we take their money.'

'What if they fight back?' Sam said. 'What if we have to kill them?'

'Then we say thank you after they're dead.'

They hopped around a bend and came in sight of the town of Backward Point. It was quite a large town, by Outfield standards. It had a whole main street, a town square, and several two-storey buildings. It used to be a gold-mining town, but nobody ever found any gold there. It used to be a farming town, but all the animals fell in the holes dug by the gold-miners. Now it survived as a market town, but today wasn't a market day, so the streets were unusually quiet.

Fred stopped at a blacksmith's on the way in, and got a large hole cut in his wombat bucket, to see and talk out of. He and Sam were just on their way out of the blacksmith's when a farmer that Fred knew happened to pass by.

'G'day, Tucker!' the farmer called. 'Nice bucket you've got there!'

Further down the street, a friend of Alice's came out of a sewing shop. 'Hello, Samantha,' she said, smiling sweetly at Sam. 'And hello, Frederick,' she said to Fred. 'What are you doing with a milking bucket on your head?'

'So much for your disguise, Dad,' Sam grumbled, as they hopped on. 'Everybody knows you here.

Maybe you should try out your master plan somewhere else.'

'Never!' Fred said.

The bank was up the far end of the street, next to one of the pubs. Outside the pub a couple of sorry-looking grey kangaroos had been tied to a post, while a stray mongrel possum had tipped over a rubbish bin, and was chewing on some old emu bones wrapped in newspaper.

The bank looked empty. They hopped up to the entrance and dismounted. Sam tied up their roos while Fred stood with his bucket jammed down tight and a boomerang in his hand, ready to burst in.

'This is it, Sam,' he said. 'Are you ready to become a legend? Are you ready to follow Mad Dog Fred Tucker to riches and glory?'

'As ready as I'll ever be,' Sam said.

'Then let's do it! On the count of three! One! Two! Hang on, my bucket's slipping . . . *Three!*'

Fred burst through the door and charged into the bank. His bucket slipped again, so that the hole for his eyes was now over his left ear, and he tripped over. He got up with the bucket turned completely the wrong way, and ran smack into a brick wall. A cuckoo clock dropped off the wall and bounced off the bucket with a loud clang.

'Crikey!' he exclaimed, swivelling the bucket around so the holes were in the right place again. 'This place is crowded! Are you with me, Sam?'

'I'm right behind you, Dad,' Sam said.

'Right! Let's get on with it!' He strode to the counter and banged on it with his fist. 'Listen up, you scumbags!' he roared. 'My name's Mad Dog Fred Tucker, the Terror of the Outfield! This is a stick-up! I've got a loaded boomerang and I'm not afraid to use it!'

He waited. Nothing happened. He peered through an open door into a small storage room beside the counter. 'Hello? Hello-o-o-o! What happened to the service around here? I said, this is a stick-up!'

A small, balding man strolled casually out of the storage room with his hands in the air. He didn't look the slightest bit scared, Sam noticed. He looked like someone who'd been held up by bushrangers many times before.

'Don't tell me, don't tell me,' he said. 'You're a goanna farmer, right? Wife and children to support. Bottom's fallen out of the goanna leather market. No, wait. I recognise the bucket. A wombat farmer. Sheesh, I might have known. What's the matter, mate, all that cheese-making cheesing you off?'

'None of your business,' Fred said. 'Are you the bank clerk?'

'No, I'm the Sugar Plum Fairy,' the bank clerk said. 'What d'you reckon?'

'Cut out the smart talk and give me all your money!' Fred demanded. 'Put it in a sack on top of the counter! And make it snappy!'

'Yeah, yeah, I've heard it all before, pal, don't worry.' The bank clerk sighed heavily, then took a large brown sack from under the counter. He stomped across to the safe, unlocked the door, and began pulling out thick piles of banknotes.

'A sack, for Pete's sake,' he muttered to himself. 'A *sack*. Who does he think he is? Santa Claus?'

He emptied the safe in double-quick time, then shut the door behind him, and dragged the sack – which was now bulging with money – back across the floor. With a tremendous heave, he hoisted it up onto the counter.

'There you go, Santa,' he said. 'I hope your reindeers are feeling frisky.'

Fred took hold of the sack. With all his strength he hauled it off the edge of the counter. He tried to sling it over his shoulder, but it was far too heavy for him. With a strangled cry he toppled over backwards, landing in a heap with the sack on top of him.

'Oh dear,' the bank clerk said. 'Santa has fallen over.'

'Crikey,' Fred said, after he had struggled free and stood up again. 'That sack weighs a ton. Our kangaroos'll never carry it. *Now* what are we going to do?'

'We could always empty some of the money out,' Sam suggested.

'Never!' Fred exclaimed. 'We need every cent we can get!'

'Then maybe we could put it into *two* sacks, and carry half each.'

'There's no time! We've got to get going!' Fred tried again to lift the sack and sling it over his shoulder, but it was no use. He stood helplessly, scratching the place on his wombat bucket where the top of his head would be.

'I wonder what Captain Toilet Light would do in this situation,' he mumbled.

'I know what *I'd* do, if I were you,' the bank clerk said, in an unexpectedly friendly tone. 'I certainly wouldn't try and make a getaway. Getaways are always so messy, don't you think? There are shoot-outs, you get chased by troopers, you're on the run for weeks at a time. Getaways are strictly for amateurs. What I would suggest is a *lot* more convenient.'

'And what might that be?' Fred asked.

'Well,' the bank clerk went on ingratiatingly 'why not open an account instead, and invest the money here with us?'

Fred blinked slowly. 'Invest the money with you?' he said. 'But I just *stole* the money from you.'

'So?' The bank clerk shrugged. 'Business is business. You're a customer, you've got money to invest, and we need more investors. Here at First Pioneer we offer a very competitive fifteen per cent interest rate for a five-year, fixed-term deposit. That way you get a good monthly income without touching your capital, and your nest-egg stays nice and safe.'

Fred stared at the bank clerk for a few more moments. Then he nodded thoughtfully. 'You know, that's not such a bad idea,' he said.

'Dad, what are you talking about?' Sam tugged at his arm. 'Don't listen to him! He's trying to trick you!'

'It's always better to save your money, rather than spend it,' the bank clerk went on. 'That's what the wise little squirrel does.'

'Dad, you can't be serious!' Sam said. 'Don't you get it? He just wants the money back! He's having you on!'

Fred smiled apologetically. 'Sorry about my daughter,' he said to the bank clerk. 'She's not a bad kid really. She just doesn't know much about money. I'm sure when she gets a bit older she'll understand.'

Sam's jaw dropped. She couldn't believe this was happening. 'Dad, no! Please!'

'Be quiet and let me handle this, Sam,' Fred said. He cleared this throat. 'I've had a chance to consider your offer, my good man,' he went on, 'and I've decided I *will* invest the money with you. In that five-term, fixed-year thingummy-whatsit you just mentioned. So let's do it! Let's open that account right now!'

He thrust an arm across the counter and shook the bank clerk's hand. As Sam watched in numb disbelief, the bank clerk reached under the counter, whipped out a form for Fred to sign, then dashed out to the sack full of stolen loot and began dragging it back towards the safe.

'An *excellent* decision, sir,' he said. 'Thank you *so* much for choosing First Pioneer. You won't regret it. We'll look after your money *very* carefully. We'll treat it *exactly* as if it were our own.'

troopers!

Ten minutes later Fred and Sam were back on their kangaroos, high-tailing it down the main street out of town.

They rode hard and fast until they got to the campsite where they had slept the night before. Fred signalled for them to stop and rest. As soon as they'd both pulled up, he whipped off his wombat bucket, waved it high above his head, and let out a tremendous whoop of triumph.

'We've done it!' he yelled. 'Our first bank job! We're rich, Sam! Rich beyond our wildest dreams!'

'But Dad, we don't have any money,' Sam said.

'Sure we do!' Fred answered. 'It's back there in the bank, getting fifteen per cent interest! We get our first payment next month!'

'There aren't going to *be* any payments,' Sam said. 'I tried to tell you earlier, but you wouldn't listen. That bank clerk pulled a fast one on you. He cheated you. He took you for every cent you had.'

Fred frowned. His mind was a strange and wonderful thing. It was a lot like quicksand. Things took a long time to sink in. And when they finally *did* sink in, they usually sank right to the bottom, and disappeared without trace.

'You mean . . . I haven't opened an account?' he asked finally.

'No,' Sam said.

'I haven't made a deposit? Into a five-term, fixed-year, nest-eggy whatchamacallit?'

'Sorry, Dad.' Sam could hardly bear to break it to him. 'The whole thing was a con-job, from start to finish.'

Fred's shoulders sagged. His jaw hung open. His whole body went slack, as if someone had opened a valve somewhere, and let all the air out of him.

'But . . . but that bank clerk was so nice!' he said weakly. 'He was so kind and helpful! If you can't trust someone like that, who *can* you trust?'

'Don't worry, Dad,' Sam said, patting him on the back. 'You did your best. But you're a wombat farmer, not a bushranger. You belong at home, milking your wombats, and making your cheese. You shouldn't be out here robbing – Dad? *Dad, where are you going?*'

Fred had wheeled Frisky around and was setting off at full gallop, back down the trail towards Backward Point.

'Nobody makes a fool out of Mad Dog Fred, the Human Feeding Frenzy!' he shouted as he sped away. 'D'you hear me? Nobody!'

Sam dug her heels into Spring's ribs, and hopped after him as fast as she could.

'Dad!' she shouted. 'Wait! You can't go back! You'll get caught!'

'Too bad!' Fred shouted. 'I'm going to give that smelly little piece of possum-poo a real roasting! And then I'm going to rob him again! Only *this* time, I'm taking the money with me!'

A cloud of dust rose behind him as he spurred Frisky on even faster. Sam was hopping at full speed, only just managing to keep up.

'You can't rob the same bank twice!' she shouted. 'Not on the same *day*!'

'Why not?' Fred said. 'Give me one good reason!'

Just as he said this, they rode over the crest of a hill and came to the head of a broad valley. Herds of goannas and hairy-nose wombats grazed peacefully in paddocks on either side of the trail. In the distance

Sam could see the town of Backward Point, no more than five kilohops away, shimmering in the noonday heat.

'You want your reason?' Sam said. 'There it is, right there.'

Not far from town was another large, billowing dust-cloud. Underneath it, thundering towards them across the plain, was a posse of six troopers. Each trooper was wearing a dark-blue uniform with a blue cap, and was mounted on a huge black thoroughbred kangaroo, nearly twice the size of Fred's and Sam's farm greys. And each, Sam could see, was carrying the deadliest weapon in the Outfield: a twin-blade, pump-action, semi-automatic boomer-rifle, far more powerful than a puny Colt .45.

'Troopers!' Fred breathed. 'But how? How could they get here so soon?'

'They must have ridden into town just after we left,' Sam said. 'They'll hang us if they catch us. We're going to have to hop for our lives!'

They wheeled their kangaroos around and began hopping at full speed away from the town. Glancing over her shoulder as she reached the crest of the hill, Sam saw to her horror that the troopers had spotted them. They were waving their boomer-rifles in the air, spurring their thoroughbreds on even faster.

Troopers like these were expert trackers. They could stay on the trail of a bushranger for months. Their leggy black kangaroos were bred especially for long-distance chases, and were much faster across open country than sturdy farm animals like Frisky and Spring.

This is it, Sam thought. *We're in deep trouble now, and no mistake. Only a miracle can save us.*

A miracle.

Sam gasped as she remembered.

The dingo! she said to herself. *Malagar! If only . . .*

But no. It would never work. To get to Malagar they had to follow the setting sun out across the open desert, perhaps for hundreds of kilohops. How were they supposed to do that with six troopers riding swift black thoroughbreds, less than five kilohops behind?

Unless . . .

She was struck suddenly by a terrific idea.

Yes, that might do it, she thought. *It's risky, very risky, but we've got no other choice.*

'They won't really hang us if they catch us, will they?' Fred said, interrupting her thoughts. 'It's not as if we actually *stole* anything. We gave all the money back. Won't they let us off with a warning?'

'They'll hang us as soon as look at us,' Sam said.

'That's their job. But listen. I think I know a way we can lose them. We have to head for Deepfry Canyon.'

'Deepfry Canyon!' Fred said. 'But that's a dead-end! Once we ride in there we're trapped! There's no way out!'

'Yes, there is,' Sam said. 'There's a path that Billy found, years ago. The troopers won't know about it. You'll have to trust me.'

Fred hesitated, then nodded. 'If Billy found it, that's good enough for me,' he said. 'Let's go.'

Soon there was no sound except for the thumping of kangaroos' paws on the ground. Sam and Fred put their heads down, stuck their bottoms in the air, and hopped like the wind.

escape from deepfry canyon

An hour later Sam and Fred were still riding. They had skirted the town of Deep Gully and were approaching the entrance to Deepfry Canyon from the north.

The troopers were still hot on their trail. Glancing over her shoulder as she crested another hill, Sam judged that they were no more than two kilohops behind. Every time she looked around, the menacing dust-cloud behind the six black thoroughbreds seemed to be drawing closer.

With a bit of luck, she and Fred could still reach Billy's path at the end of Deepfry Canyon. Billy had found this path one afternoon when he and Sam were in the canyon mustering wombats. He had noticed a pile of boulders from a recent rock-slide, stacked against the sheer canyon wall. Before Sam could stop him he was off, guiding his kangaroo over the boulders, trying to find a way to the top.

Nobody had ever ridden up the side of Deepfry Canyon before. Billy wanted to be the first, so he could boast about it to his mates at the next roo-deo. Up and up he went, higher and higher, urging his kangaroo from rock to rock. Eventually he got so high, and the path underneath him grew so narrow, that Sam couldn't watch. She hid her face in her hands, and didn't look up again until Billy hollered down that he was safe.

Now Sam and Fred would have to take exactly the same path. Their farm kangaroos could never outrun the troopers' thoroughbreds, but they could certainly outclimb them. Sam knew very well that thoroughbreds were nervous creatures who didn't like heights. If her hunch was correct, they would refuse to follow Frisky and Spring up over the boulders. This might just give her and Fred enough time to get away.

The question is, will Frisky and Spring be willing to climb that high? Sam wondered. *And if they are, can they climb fast enough to escape the troopers' guns?*

The boomer-rifles carried by the troopers were awesome weapons. They were shaped like cross-bows, and fired deadly, metal-tipped, twin-blade boomerangs automatically, at the press of a trigger. They had a range of more than a hundred metres, and a direct hit even from that distance could smash a rock.

If the troopers get close enough to start shooting, we're history, Sam thought. *They'll pound us into a boomerang meringue.*

As soon as they entered the canyon the sunlight disappeared, blotted out by steep granite walls on either side. 'So where's this path Billy found?' Fred called.

'It's right at the end of the canyon,' Sam called back. 'Another four kilohops.'

'You're kidding!' Fred looked fearfully over his shoulder. 'We'll never make it! They're gaining too fast!'

'The canyon'll slow them down,' Sam said. 'We'll make it. Just keep hopping.'

On they went. The canyon walls grew higher, the floor narrower, and the shadows around them gloomier. Frisky and Spring were tiring now, but they seemed to sense how important it was to keep going.

'There!' Sam called out eventually, pointing up ahead to where the canyon ended at a dried-up water-fall. 'There's the path!'

Just before the waterfall the canyon grew suddenly wide again, and was once more bathed in sunshine. The rockslide was a couple of hundred hops to Sam's left.

'What path?' Fred peered ahead in confusion. 'All I see is a rock-slide. I don't see any path.'

'The rock-slide *is* the path!' Sam said. 'We go up it! We hop from rock to rock!'

Fred stared at the rock-slide, stunned. 'Where I come from,' he said hoarsely, 'we don't call that a path. We call that a *cliff*.'

'Billy rode up there,' Sam insisted. 'I watched him. Come on, Dad. If he can do it, we can too.'

'You see, Sam,' Fred went on, without missing a beat, 'a *path* goes along the ground. It's flat, and sometimes it's got trees on either side of it, or benches to have picnics on, or pretty flowers growing along the edge. A path does *not* go straight up in the air. When it goes straight up in the air, it's called a *cliff*. And if you think I'm going to try and ride my kangaroo up this *cliff*,' Fred concluded, still staring upwards, 'you are out of your teeny little mind.'

Just then, from off in the distance back up the canyon, there came a rumbling of galloping kangaroos. Sam and Fred stared at each other, wide-eyed.

'Follow me!' Sam shouted. 'Come on, Spring, take us up! Go!'

Spring didn't need to be told twice. In a single

bound he leapt to the top of the nearest boulder, carrying Sam up with him. Frisky did the same. Fred immediately threw his arms tight around Frisky's neck, and shut his eyes.

'No-o-o-o!!' he howled. 'Oxygen! I can't breathe! It's too high! We're all going to die!'

'Don't look down, Dad,' Sam said. 'We'll make it if we stay calm. Just don't look down.'

'Don't look down,' Fred muttered to himself. 'Okay. That's easy if I keep my eyes closed. I know – I'll sing a song to myself. *Rock-a-bye baby, on the treetop . . . when the wind blows, the . . .* No! Not that one! That's a falling-down song! Sing a staying-on-your-kangaroo song, quick! *Oh give me a ho-o-me, where the kangaroos ro-o-am, and the snakes and scorpions play-y-y-y-y . . .*'

The rumble of the thoroughbreds grew louder. They were surely only a few hundred hops away now. Sam was climbing far too fast, taking terrible risks as she steered Spring from boulder to boulder. They *had* to stay out of range of those boomer-rifles. Otherwise they would be blown to smithereens.

'Halfway,' she muttered grimly, a short time afterwards. She paused, glancing upwards at the treacherous ascent that lay ahead. 'Good boy, Spring. Keep it up. Dad, how are you going?'

'*I'm a little teapot, short and stout. Here is my handle, here is my——*'

At that moment the six troopers burst out into the sunlight. They spread out for a moment, confused, then re-gathered as their sergeant – a short, bulldoggish man with tiny, cruel eyes and a thick moustache – spotted their prey. A sharp command rang out. All six troopers drew their rifles. They wheeled around and headed for the base of the rock-slide as fast as they could.

'They're coming!' Fred wailed. 'This is not good! *This is not good!*'

'Keep climbing!' Sam urged, zig-zagging her way up a steep slope of loose rock and gravel like a skier skiing the wrong way. 'We're nearly there! A few dozen more hops!'

As she spoke, Sam heard a strange whistling noise. It sounded close and far away, both at the same time. All at once there was a tremendous explosion off to her right. A spray of loose stones began rolling and bouncing down the cliff.

'They're shooting!' Fred yelled. 'Take cover! Duck and weave! Women and children first!'

Another twin-blade boomerang whistled past on Sam's left. It sent sparks flying as it crashed against a rock. After that the boomerangs came thick and fast, not accurate yet, but still much too close for comfort. They were beginning to break up the rock-slide. More and more stones – and even some large boulders – were clattering and lumbering away down the cliff.

'The whole lot's going!' Sam yelled. 'Hurry, Dad, hurry!'

They pressed on. The explosions grew nearer, and more numerous. All at once, just as it seemed that one more direct hit would bring the entire cliff-face crashing to the ground, the firing stopped.

Sam was only seconds from the top. Fred was one or two hops behind, still clutching Frisky tightly around the neck, while Frisky picked his way up the slope.

'They're not shooting,' Fred said suddenly, and sat up. 'They're not shooting! Ha! They must have run out of boomerangs!'

'No, I don't think so.' Sam glanced down. 'I think they're coming up after us. They don't want to destroy the path.'

Sam was right. At a command from the sergeant, all six of the troopers had held their fire. They had gathered at the base of the cliff, and were urging their thoroughbreds to jump onto the first boulder.

The thoroughbreds were terrified. The more their

riders cursed them and whipped them and kicked them, the more steadfastly they refused to jump.

'They won't climb!' Sam breathed a long sigh of relief, then clenched her fist in triumph. '*Yes!* We've beaten them! We're going to make it!'

A few moments later Spring made the last, difficult jump from the loose gravel at the top of the rock-slide onto solid ground at the top of the canyon. Sam looked back, expecting to see her father following close behind – but Fred had stopped. He'd taken a boomerang out of his holster and was waving it gleefully at the troopers.

'Cowards!' he shouted down. 'Too scared to shoot, eh? Well I'm not! This is Mad Dog Fred Tucker talking, the Terror of the Outfield! You see this throwing arm? It's insured for twenty million dollars! One more hop and I'll send a red-hot Colt .45 down to chop off your short and curlies!'

'Dad, are you crazy!' Sam hissed. 'Get up here, quick!'

'What's the matter, boys, can't you climb?' Fred went on. 'You big bunch of pansies! It's easy! It's a stroll in the park! My grandma could do it riding on her possum!'

This was too much for the trooper sergeant. Scowling furiously, he raised his boomer-rifle to his shoulder and fired. The boomerang skimmed towards Fred in a deadly arc, missing him by millihops. It exploded into the hillside, sending Fred and Frisky tumbling sideways down the slope.

With a rumble that turned rapidly to a roar, the entire rock-slide began to give way.

'Uh-oh,' Fred said, as the ground trembled underneath him. 'Why am I getting this sinking feeling –'

'Get up!' Sam shouted. 'Run! It's collapsing!'

Frisky was on his feet again in an instant. He bounded forward nimbly over the slowly moving tide of loose gravel, and made it to the top in a flash. Fred, however, was left floundering five or six hops below, lurching and staggering like a drunken man. Every time he took a step forward he was swept back just as far by the continuous downward flow of the stones.

Leaping off Spring's back, Sam took a rope from her saddlebag. She looped one end around the kangaroo's middle, then threw the other end off the top of the cliff to Fred. The rumble of falling rocks was deafening now. The troopers were retreating as fast as they could. Fred grasped hold of Sam's rope just as the rock-slide finally gave way. He suddenly found himself swinging in mid-air, with his feet scrabbling against the sheer side of the cliff. Spring braced and held firm. Straining with all his might, he hauled Fred to the top of the cliff and safety.

'Crikey,' Fred gasped, as he collapsed on the ground beside Sam. 'I thought you said they wouldn't shoot.'

When the avalanche had finally settled, Fred and Sam got down on their knees, and peered over the edge. All that remained of the rock-slide was a giant heap of rubble. The troopers were picking their way amongst the boulders on their kangaroos, searching in vain for another path.

One of the troopers spotted them, and took aim.

'There they are, sir!' he called to the trooper sergeant. 'At the top of the cliff! Permission to blow their heads off, sir!'

'Hold your fire, corporal, hold your fire.' The trooper sergeant scowled up at Fred and Sam, then spat in the dirt. 'I suppose you're pretty pleased with yourself, aren't you, Mad Dog?' he called up. 'You might even think you've got away. Well, let me ask you just one question. Where do you plan on going?'

Fred was about to answer when Sam dug him in the ribs. He stayed quiet.

'Wherever you go, whatever you do, you're going to leave tracks,' the trooper sergeant went on. 'And I promise you, we'll find those tracks. We'll follow you to the ends of the earth if we have to. We'll keep coming till you drop dead from exhaustion, then we'll hang you from the nearest tree till your face turns blue and the crows peck out your eyes. We never let a bushranger get away, Mad Dog. Never. So enjoy the view, my friend. It's not going to last.'

With that he wheeled around and galloped off back down the canyon. The rest of the troopers followed close behind him, boomer-rifles raised in the air, whooping and hollering.

into the 8 desert

'I reckon we've got about two hours start on them,' Sam said a short time later, as they were sitting at the top of the cliff trying to decide what to do. 'It'll be dark before long. They can't follow us then. But as soon as the sun comes up, they'll be right back on our trail.'

'You know any more rock-slides we can climb?' Fred said.

'Nope,' Sam said.

'Right. We're stuffed then.' Fred looked crestfallen. 'You saw how fast those thoroughbreds are. They'll catch us tomorrow for sure.'

'Maybe. Maybe not.' Sam got to her feet. Shielding her eyes, she gazed westward into the desert. Below her was a vast wilderness of stones and boulders, cracked red earth, spinifex grasses, acacia trees, and thorns. Strange misshapen red hills rose up from the plains like giant termite mounds. The late afternoon sun covered the entire landscape in a baking, shimmering heat.

'D'you believe in miracles, Dad?' she asked.

'Eh?' Fred said. 'Miracles? Sure I believe in miracles. You see them stuck to the bottom of fishing boats all the time.'

'Those are *barnacles*, Dad,' Sam said with a sigh. 'Miracles are—— Oh, never mind. I guess you don't believe in talking dingoes, either.'

Fred peered at her suspiciously. 'There was a talking dingo at a puppet show we went to once,' he said. 'And *you* told me it wasn't real.'

Sam tried a more direct approach. 'I think we should head out into the desert,' she said. 'Maybe we can hide somewhere out there, and throw the troopers off our trail.'

Fred looked aghast. 'But I hate the desert!' he said. 'It's full of crawley, bitey things! Why can't we head for the coast, and hide in the surf?'

'That's what the troopers will *expect* us to do,' Sam said. 'And besides,' she added mysteriously, 'if we go into the desert, there's a chance we might find something ve-e-ery interesting.'

'Really?' Fred perked up. 'Like what? A dead emu?'

'No. A tree. A *sacred* tree. It's the secret entrance to a place called Malagar. Have you ever heard of it?'

Fred shook his head.

'It's a place from a story Mum used to tell me,' Sam said. 'I never used to think it was real. But I met someone who came from there, and he gave me directions. He said if we were ever in desperate trouble, he would help us. And I don't reckon trouble gets any more desperate than this.'

Fred didn't look convinced. 'Sounds like a long shot to me,' he said. 'I've never heard of any towns out in the middle of the desert. It's just desert, all the way to China.'

'But Malagar isn't a *town*,' Sam said. 'It's a lost paradise, hidden from the outside world by magic, and ruled over by the Great Dingo.'

Fred perked up all of a sudden. 'Did you say . . . *great* dingo?' he said. '*How* great? Bigger than our farm kangaroos?'

'Probably,' Sam shrugged. 'I don't know.'

Big enough to make *two* pairs of slippers?' Fred said. '*And* a rug?'

'I don't think——' Sam began. Then she hesitated. 'Sure, Dad,' she said. 'Maybe even *three* pairs of slippers. Who knows?'

'*Three pairs of slippers!*' Fred leapt to his feet, hunting instincts roused. 'That's it! What are we waiting for? Let's go-o-o-o!'

They packed their saddlebags and gave the kangaroos a drink from their small store of water. Then they set off. Riding down the western slope of the ridge was a lot easier than climbing up the rock-slide. It wasn't nearly so steep, and there were clear trails left by wild broncaroos and free-ranging wombats. They soon reached the bottom, and set out across the desert.

'We have to follow the setting sun until we find the Sacred Tree,' Sam said. 'That means we go . . . this way.' She checked her compass. 'West-south-west.'

They hopped at a good speed until it got dark. Sam insisted they keep going, right through the night, using the compass to guide them. When morning came again, they found they had left the flat plains country. Not far ahead of them was an area of long, low ridges sweeping from north to south, dotted with strange red mounds like those Sam had seen from the top of the canyon. It was much better country to hide in, and Sam's spirits lifted considerably.

Behind her, Fred was flopping on Frisky's back like a rag doll. 'Slee-e-e-ep,' he moaned. 'Must have sle-e-e-ep.'

'We'll stop just ahead,' Sam said. 'There should be some shade on one of those hills, maybe even a cave we can sleep in. Keep a look out for water, too, we've only got enough for two more days.'

'How close are the troopers?' Fred asked blearily.

'I'm not sure,' Sam said. 'It depends how far they rode last night. But we can't go any further, no matter how close they are. We've got to rest.'

They soon reached one of the giant red mounds, which was as tall and wide as a castle. Sam dismounted, and went to have a scout around. As she climbed the side of the hill, she surveyed the country further to the west, looking for something that might help them; some way of throwing the troopers off their trail.

What if the troopers have ridden all night as well? she asked herself. *They'll only be an hour away, maybe even less. Oh well, we'll just have to chance it.*

There was a cave near the top of the hill, on the western side. It was big enough for the two of them, their kangaroos, and all their gear. It was cool and dry inside, and not too uncomfortable, in the middle of the soft dirt floor.

Fred fell asleep on his blanket almost as soon as he lay down on it. Sam stayed awake a while longer, thinking of Billy and her mother back home.

When she finally drifted off, a picture floated into her mind. It was a picture of a beautiful place that she had never seen before. Towering bush-covered hills rose up behind lush rainforests. Clear mountain streams tumbled over magnificent waterfalls and swirled through enormous caverns lit by glow-worms. On the bank of one of these streams, high up in the mountains, was the dingo Sam had rescued. It was standing on two legs, with its arms folded, staring at her as if to say, 'What's keeping you, kid? I haven't got all day.'

snakes  alive

Sam woke with a start after a short, restless sleep. She sat up quickly. She had a terrible feeling that something was wrong.

A noise had woken her. Not a loud noise, but a creepy, dry rustling sound, like something slithering across the dirt floor. It couldn't have been Frisky and Spring. They were standing motionless in the corner of the cave . . .

Then she saw it.

She screamed.

An enormous desert python had slithered into the cave, and was wrapping itself around her father.

The python was easily large enough to swallow a person. It had already wound itself around most of Fred's body, from his knees right up to his shoulders.

Now its head was hovering directly above his face. It was flicking its long forked tongue at his nose.

Fred was still fast asleep. Each time the python's tongue tickled his nose, he jerked his head back sharply. Sam thought about calling out to him, but she didn't want to do anything that might make the python panic and tighten its grip.

The python opened its massive jaws. To Sam's horror, it began swallowing Fred's head.

Fred stirred drowsily. 'Hmm?' he muttered. 'Alice? Izzat you? Woss going on?'

'Dad!' Sam hissed. 'Dad, wake up! You're being eaten!'

It was no use. The jaws were now covering Fred's ears. He couldn't hear her properly. Her mind raced as she tried to decide what to do. Boomerangs were no good: she couldn't throw a boomerang inside a cave this small. She could stab the python with her bush-knife, but it was packed away in her saddlebag, on Spring's back. By the time she got it out and came back, her father would be dead.

She did the only thing she could do. She grabbed a rock from the floor of the cave, and brought it down hard on the tip of the python's tail.

The python stiffened. It hissed loudly in pain, but instead of letting Fred go, it wound its coils around him even more tightly, and pushed its jaws further over his head.

'Whoa!' Fred said, in a voice even more muffled than before. 'Steady on there, Alice! I've heard of French kissing, but this is ridiculous!'

'Dad, wake up!' Sam yelled again. 'It's a python! You're being eaten alive!'

She was now whacking at the python's tail with the rock as hard as she could. The python did not like this one little bit. It began thrashing from side to side, bouncing and bucking Fred all over the floor, but never lessening its grip on him for an instant.

'Oh yeah!' Fred exclaimed. 'Hot stuff, baby! Show me what love is!'

'*Dad, it's not Mum, it's a python!*' Sam shrieked. '*It's swallowing you! Do something, quick!*'

Fred finally realised what was happening. He bit down on the python's tonsil, as hard as he could. The python hissed and thrashed about like a mad thing. It wasn't used to being bitten on the tonsil by its breakfast. Normally breakfast gave a few timid squeaks, then gave up and let itself be swallowed. But not this time.

With a choking, spluttering cough, the snake opened its jaws and regurgitated Fred's head.

'Phew!' Fred exclaimed, blowing a big blob of

snake-spit off his nose. 'A python, eh? I guess that explains the bad breath.'

'It's crushing you!' Sam wailed. 'I can't stop it! I can't get it off!'

The python still had its coils wound around Fred. It had given up trying to eat him alive, and was now hell-bent on crushing him to death. Every time Fred let out a breath, the python contracted its coils. It tightened them a little bit at a time, but soon the pressure on Fred's lungs was so great that he couldn't breathe.

'Help! Sam!' he gasped. 'I'm dying! Get it . . . off me!'

Sam was desperate. She kept whacking at the python with her rock. She tugged at its tail. She grabbed its head, and tried to poke out its eyes. But the python wasn't giving up. It was only a few seconds away from enjoying the biggest meal of its life, and nothing Sam could do was going to stop it now.

'I'm trying, Dad, I'm trying!' Sam cried. 'But it's no use!'

Fred's face had gone purple. His eyes were rolling. Just then, at the very moment when all hope seemed lost, *another* giant desert python slithered into the cave.

This second python was even bigger than the

first. What's more, the cave was actually on its territory. When it saw that an intruder had snaked inside, and was about to help itself to a free bushranger, it did what any red-blooded giant desert python would have done.

It attacked.

The python that was crushing Fred suddenly let go. It reared up, hissing, facing its attacker. The two snakes lunged, twisting and biting with all their might. First one of them was on top, then the other one. It was soon impossible to tell which snake was which. Watching them fight was a bit like watching two very large and colourful fire hoses getting tumbled in a spin-dryer. Faster and faster they writhed, getting more and more frenzied and tangled and intertwined.

The fight continued for a full five minutes. At the end of that time the two snakes had become so horribly tangled and knotted and intertwined that they couldn't move.

Sam and Fred couldn't believe it. The two snakes were literally knotted solid, right there in front of them.

'They're stuck!' Fred said. 'Look at them, Sam! They can't get untied!'

He gave a half-demented laugh of relief, then danced triumphantly across to the bizarre-looking python-ball in the middle of the floor. Keeping well clear of the two hissing heads protruding from the top, he gave the ball a shove.

'Thought you'd try and eat me, eh?' he taunted. 'Well, I guess you bit off more than you could chew, didn't you? This'll teach you to mistake my head for a Chuba-chub! You won't mess with Mad Dog Fred Tucker again in a hurry!'

He turned to Sam and grinned. 'What a story!' he said. 'Wait till I tell everyone back home! I might even set it to music . . . yes, that's it! I'll write a ballad! "The Ballad of Mad Dog Fred Tucker and the Giant Desert Pythons!" It'll sell a mint!'

'Later, Dad,' Sam said 'We've got to get going.'

As quickly as she could, Sam rolled up her blanket and packed it away in her saddlebag. She did the same thing to Fred's blanket, which was now extremely rumpled-looking, and badly smeared with dirt. Fred, meanwhile, had wandered off with a thoughtful look on his face, and was scratching his chin.

'What rhymes with "python"?' he said to himself. 'Dython? No, that's no good. Kython? Smython?'

Sam left him to compose his ballad, and went outside. She climbed quickly to the top of the hill, keeping to the western side so she wouldn't be seen by anyone approaching from the east. She swept her eyes back across the plains, checking the path she and her father had taken the night before.

There it was. A dust-cloud, no more than a speck on the horizon, fifteen kilohops distant. The troopers would be here in an hour.

Sam's heart fell. It was useless to run. She and her father simply couldn't travel fast enough. They would be caught before the end of the day, and hung, unless she could think of a way to throw the troopers off the trail.

We could cover our tracks by wading in a creek, she thought. *But there are no creeks for hundreds of kilohops, in any direction. Maybe we could wipe the tracks away with something? A tree branch, tied to the kangaroos' tails? No, that's too obvious.*

What else, then? What else could she do?

Sam scrambled back down to the cave. If only they could leave *different* tracks. The tracks of some other animal, besides a kangaroo. Python tracks would be perfect. They would bamboozle the troopers completely. But neither Sam nor her father had ever learnt to ride pythons, so that was no good either . . .

Then, all of a sudden, it hit her.

She caught sight of her father and the two pythons again, and was struck by another wonderful idea.

a very winding trail

Sam had had a lot of good ideas in her short but colourful life. Mostly they related to wombats, and how to milk them, or muster them, or shear them, or teach them to sit up and beg. But she had never had an idea as good as this. It was an absolute gem.

She didn't waste too much time thinking about it. As soon as she had made up her mind that it would work, she snapped into action.

'Dad, listen,' she said to her father. 'The troopers are coming. I saw them. They'll be here in less than an hour. I want you to come here and knock out these two pythons, so we can untangle them, and tie them to our kangaroos' tails.'

Fred looked horrified. 'What?' he said. '*Untangle* them? Are you crazy?'

'Dad, please,' Sam said. 'There's not much time. You need to do exactly as I say.'

Fred frowned so deeply that his forehead almost folded in half. 'You want me to knock out the two pythons?' he repeated, in a thoroughly baffled voice. 'So we can untangle them, and tie them to our kangaroos' tails? Why on earth would we want to do that?'

'So the snakes will slither behind us when we ride away from here!' Sam said. 'They'll wipe out our *roo* tracks with their *snake* tracks, and the troopers won't follow *snake* tracks, because they'll be looking for *roos*!'

Her father looked more confused than ever. 'You want to run that past me again?' he said. 'I think I might have missed a bit.'

'If we tie the pythons behind our kangaroos,' Sam said slowly, 'they'll leave *snake* tracks when we're riding away. Snake tracks instead of roo tracks. And that will fool the troopers. Don't you see?'

Finally it sank in. '*Snake* tracks!' Fred exclaimed. 'Instead of . . . ! To cover the . . . ! Holy Hairy-Nose, it's brilliant, Sam! It's the best idea I've ever heard!'

'We'll have to tie the snakes on backwards, so they don't bite the kangaroos' tails,' Sam went on. 'That shouldn't matter. Snakes ought to leave the same trail going backwards as they do forwards.'

'I don't think I've ever seen a snake going back-wards,' Fred said thoughtfully.

'They must go backwards *sometimes*,' Sam said. 'When they get stuck down a hole, or wedged under a rock.'

'Yeah,' Fred nodded. 'Or when they're reversing into a park.'

'And they'd still have to slither, wouldn't they?' Sam said. 'So their tracks would *have* to be the same. Or close enough so the troopers would never tell the difference.'

'And they'll go round and round in circles looking for roo tracks, when we'll be long gone! It's fantastic!' Fred gazed at his daughter in rapt admiration. 'You're a genius, Sam,' he said. 'Maybe *you* should be the bushranger and I should be the backside-kicker from now on. How about that?'

'That's sidekick, Dad,' Sam said. 'But no, I'm a wombat farmer. And so are you.'

Fred ignored this comment. Whistling cheerfully, he approached the tangled ball of snakes. He lined up the nearest head, then let fly with a tremendous right hook. The punch landed flush on the underside of the python's jaw, knocking it senseless. He finished off the second python with exactly the same punch, then joined Sam in untangling them.

This was no easy task. Imagine untangling two shoelaces the size of fire-hoses that you've accidentally knotted together. Or imagine untangling two *real* fire-hoses that you've accidentally knotted together, while a couple of beefy firemen stand over you with their arms folded, waiting to put out the fire.

It took Sam and Fred half an hour. As soon as they had finished Sam grabbed her bush-knife and her rope from her saddlebag. She cut the rope into two even lengths, then used each length to tie a python to a kangaroo, tail to tail.

Frisky and Spring did not like this one bit. They liked it even less when the pythons began to stir, and hiss quietly. By that time Fred and Sam had saddled up and were ready to leave. They set off out of the cave and down the hillside as fast as they could.

The pythons were wide awake in an instant. They twisted and bucked and thrashed about with all their might. But Frisky and Spring had been trained to pull fenceposts, and fallen trees, and many other things heavier things than desert pythons. They took no notice.

'Get to the nearest ridge, and stay behind it,' Sam said. She pointed to a long, low hill that rose up out of the desert just ahead. 'We'll have to head south for a while. The troopers will track our roos into the cave, but they won't see any roo tracks coming out again. With a bit of luck they might think we got eaten by the pythons.'

The pythons were still trying to slither in the opposite direction to the kangaroos. But no matter how hard they fought, and how much they twisted and hissed and thrashed about, Frisky and Spring kept on dragging them backwards. After a minute or two they took the easy option, and let themselves be dragged. They relaxed and started slithering backwards as though it was the most natural thing in the world.

'Perfect snake trails,' Sam said proudly, as she admired the winding, curving tracks the snakes were now leaving behind.

'No sign of roo prints anywhere,' Fred said.

'You'd never know we were here,' Sam said.

'This is going to sound great in the ballad,' Fred said. 'As soon as I find something to rhyme with "python".'

They hopped with the snakes slithering behind them for two more hours, keeping behind ridges and hills all the while. This took them way off course, but Sam wasn't worried. As soon as it was dark she would use her compass and start heading west-south-west towards the setting sun. For now the most important thing was to stay low.

Late in the morning Sam noticed that the two pythons had almost stopped moving. Their bodies had gone limp, and their heads were dragging on the ground, bumping over rocks and stones. 'I think those snakes have slithered their last slither,' she said to Fred. 'They're just plumb slithered out.'

The two pythons were in a very sorry state. It's one thing to slither backwards out from under a rock from time to time. It's quite another to slither backwards over open desert for two hours, towed by a determined kangaroo. No snake in history had ever slithered backwards that far, or that fast. If there was a Guinness Book of Records for snakes, those two plucky desert pythons would get a full page in the 'Feats of Endurance' section, all to themselves.

Sam stopped and cut them loose. They lay there, twitching and hissing faintly.

'They'll recover soon enough,' Sam said. She got out her water-bottle and took a small sip, then gave another sip to her father. After that she poured a few mouthfuls into two shallow bowls, which she gave to Frisky and Spring.

'Let's hope we find that Sacred Tree soon,' she said, as she returned the water-bottle to her saddlebag. 'Or the troopers won't *have* to hang us. We'll die of thirst all by ourselves.'

the sacred tree

It was hot.

It was so hot that even the rocks had blisters.

It was so hot that a goanna sunbaking on a sand-hill had passed out, and was beginning to sizzle.

It was so hot that emu eggs were cracking open in their nests, and frying themselves.

Sam and Fred had left the hill country behind and entered the deep desert. The land ahead of them was as flat and smooth and scorched as a frying pan. The heat ballooned up around them, covering every-thing in a shifting, glistening haze.

From time to time they thought they saw some-thing up ahead – a hill, or a boulder, or a tree, or even a lake. But when they got close, the object they had seen began to bend and change shape in front of them. One moment it looked far away. Then it looked close. Then, when they reached the place where they were sure it must be, it wasn't there at all.

Sam had heard of mirages, of course, and understood that that was what she was looking at. But she had never realised they could seem so *real*.

Frisky and Spring had hopped magnificently, but they were finally beginning to falter. They were going more slowly now than when they'd dragged the two pythons, and getting slower all the time. Sam and Fred urged them on, but it was no good. They were reaching the very end of their strength.

'We'd better walk them,' Sam said. She stopped and dismounted. Fred reluctantly did the same. They each took another sip of water – their last till sundown – and trudged on.

Sam began to feel desperately weary and thirsty. Her tongue swelled up like a puffer-fish inside her mouth. Her throat felt as though it was lined with sandpaper, and her eyes were smarting so badly she could hardly keep them open.

Fred was in an even worse state. His face was brick-red, his lips were cracked, and his eyes had taken on a dazed, faraway look. He was singing softly to himself to keep up his spirits, but he couldn't seem to remember which song he was singing.

'*Oh give me a home* . . .' he warbled, in a high, cracked voice, '*short and stout . . . and down will come baby . . . among the gum trees* . . .'

All at once he stopped. He let go of Frisky's reins and went stumbling blindly across the desert. Sam called to him, but he kept going, his mouth open and his arms outstretched like a zombie's.

'There it is, Sam!' he cried. 'Up ahead! Oh, it's beautiful!'

Sam squinted. All she could see was cracked red earth and heat shimmers.

'What?' she said. 'Dad, wait! What are you looking at?'

'What am I *looking* at?' Fred was incredulous. 'Can't you *see*? It's the Taj Mahal! India at last!'

He fell to his knees, then got up again and began running, almost tripping over himself in his eagerness to reach the mirage. To Sam's horror, he began stripping off his clothes. He tore off his sweaty, dirt-stained leather jerkin and tossed it behind him. Then he began fumbling with the buttons on his shirt.

'Fountains!' he cried. 'Lakes! Sprinklers! Water-slides! It's like Wet & Wild with elephants!'

Sam sprinted after him and tackled him just as he was starting to take off his trousers. With his pants down around his knees, he quickly crashed to the ground. The impact jolted him back to his senses. He lifted his head and gave Sam a puzzled look.

'Where am I?' he said. 'What am I doing with my pants down?'

'You're undressing,' Sam explained. 'To play under the sprinklers.'

'The *sprinklers*?' Fred frowned, and got to his feet to do up his fly. 'Come on, Sam. We're in the middle of the desert. I think you've had a touch too much sun.'

When Fred was dressed, he tried to walk back to Frisky, but he soon sank to his knees again. 'I've had it, Sam,' he said. 'I'm done in. I can't go on any longer.'

'Sure you can,' Sam said. She took his arm and helped him up. 'We've still got some water left. You'll be fine after you drink that. Just think of Mum and Billy and the wombat farm, waiting for us back home.'

Fred managed a weak smile. 'D'you know, Sam,' he said as he stumbled painfully on, 'I don't think I want to be a bushranger any more. All this getting shot at, and escaping from troopers, and being swallowed by pythons, it's more than a man can bear. All I want to do is go home and farm my wombats again. I want to hear the sound of the galahs screeching outside my window in the mornings. The noise of the kangaroos stamping, and the wombats mooing gently in the paddocks. The smell of your mother's wombat rissoles sizzling in the pan. The sound of Billy lying doing nothing in his bedroom. There's no place like home, isn't that right, Sam?'

'It sure is,' Sam said. 'And we'll see it again soon, Dad. I promise.'

'I doubt that very much, young lady.' A harsh, sneering voice rang out behind them. Sam and Fred spun around to see the trooper sergeant no more than ten hops away, mounted on his thoroughbred. Beside him was his squad of troopers. All six of them had crept up so quietly that Sam and Fred hadn't heard a thing. Their boomer-rifles were raised, loaded, and ready to fire.

'We meet again, Mad Dog,' the trooper sergeant said. 'I told you we never let a bushranger get away. Now take your boomerangs out of your holsters, and lay them on the ground. Nice and slow.'

'Don't do it, Sam,' Fred whispered. 'I know they look real, but actually they're just a figment of our imaginations.'

'I don't think so, Dad,' Sam whispered back. 'They look pretty real to me.'

'It's just the heat playing tricks on us,' Fred went

on. 'Look, I'll prove it. I'll walk right up to them, and make them disappear.'

He stepped forward. Instantly the trooper sergeant fired. A deadly, metal-tipped, twin-blade boomerang zinged past Fred's ear.

'Yikes!' Fred said. 'This mirage is loaded!'

'The only reason I didn't blast your head off, Mad Dog,' the trooper sergeant growled, 'is that I want the pleasure of seeing you hang. Now, get those boomerangs on the ground and your hands in the air, and make it snappy!'

Sam and Fred did as they were told. The trooper sergeant dismounted, and came forward to collect the weapons. He began walking in a slow circle around Fred and Sam, gloating over his prize.

'I bet you thought you'd got away, didn't you, Mad Dog?' he sneered. 'I have to admit, you came pretty close. I still don't know how you fooled us, back at that cave. We couldn't find your prints anywhere. For a while we thought we'd lost you completely. But none of that matters now. What matters is that I guessed where you were going.'

'How did you do that?' Sam asked.

The trooper sergeant smiled at her smugly. 'You're not the only one with a compass,' he said. 'Ever since you left Deepfry Canyon you've been heading west-south-west. You've gone in a dead straight line, never once altering course. So I guessed that sooner or later you'd start heading that way again. And I was right, wasn't I?'

Sam's heart fell. It was so simple. So obvious. How could she not have thought of it? She stared at the ground in front of her, feeling stupider than she'd ever felt in her life. 'Sorry, Dad,' she said.

'No worries, Sam,' Fred replied. 'These troopers aren't really going to hang us. They're nice men who are just trying to teach us a lesson. Any minute now they're going to pardon us, and tell us all is forgiven, and send us on our way home with a complimentary fridge magnet and a box of chocolates. You wait and see.'

'Get out the hanging ropes!' The trooper sergeant shouted. 'And march them to the old dead tree! They die at noon!'

'But . . . but you can't do this!' Fred spluttered. 'You're making a big mistake! I'm not really Mad Dog Fred! I mean, I *was* Mad Dog Fred, sure, for a little while there. I tried to hold up a bank, it's true, but that was two whole days ago! My life's changed since then! I've given up bushranging and gone back to being plain old Fred Tucker, a poor-but-honest wombat farmer——'

'Save it for your tombstone, Mad Dog,' the trooper sergeant snarled. 'Your pathetic excuses won't wash with me. You've been tried and found guilty of robbery with violence, resisting arrest, wearing a stupid-looking bucket on your head, escaping from a canyon, and disappearing from a cave. You are hereby sentenced to hang by the neck until dead.'

'I've been sentenced?' Fred said in surprise. 'When was my trial?'

'Just then,' the trooper sergeant said. 'I tried you myself. I don't need judges and juries and all that sissy kind of stuff. Now get moving!'

Fred and Sam stumbled back the way they had come, still with their hands raised in the air. The trooper sergeant got back on his thoroughbred and hopped slowly along beside them, aiming his boomer-rifle at them all the while.

'Bring their kangaroos!' he ordered one of his men. 'We'll need them for the hanging too! Any last requests, Mad Dog, before justice prevails?'

'If you could let me scratch my nose, that'd be nice,' Fred said.

'That's typical of you bushrangers,' the trooper sergeant snarled. 'Defiant to the last. You've led us a merry dance, Mad Dog. You were cleverer than most, but now the jig is up. The curtain's drawn. The party's over. The ref's blown his whistle and the fat lady's sung her last song. You're going to burn in Hell!'

Fred and Sam marched on, under the blazing sun. After a short while a hidden valley appeared suddenly in front of them. At first Sam thought it was a mirage, but as she got closer, and the land began to slope down into it, she realised it wasn't.

In the middle of the valley, surrounded by cracked red earth, stood a very striking dead tree. It was tall and gnarled and spreading, like a fig tree. From its trunk a hundred branches sprouted, and none of them bore a single leaf. The entire tree was completely bare. It wasn't the usual colour of a dead tree, but an eerie, ghostly white. It looked as though it had been coated with whitewash, or covered in a permanent, glistening frost.

What Sam saw next made her heart leap.

A dozen dingoes were gathered underneath the tree's branches.

It's the Sacred Tree! she thought. *We passed only a few hundred hops away from it, and never saw it! But here it is!*

Her mind raced. She tried desperately to remember what the dingo had told her, about finding the Secret Door. There didn't seem to be any kind of door anywhere, certainly not in the trunk of the tree, or cut into the ground nearby.

One of the troopers fired his rifle in warning. The mob of dingoes scattered in panic.

Stand in the shadow of the tree when shadows die, Sam remembered, *and the Secret Door will open.*

She looked again. There was a shadow under the Sacred Tree, cast by the branches. No problem there. But how could a shadow be dead? Did that mean it would disappear? If it did, how were they supposed to stand in it?

None of it made any sense at all.

'Right, men!' the trooper sergeant shouted, interrupting her thoughts. 'It's nearly noon! You know your jobs! Let's get this hanging organised!'

At once the five other men dismounted, and set to work. Two of them began knotting a hangman's noose in each of the hanging ropes. One more went to the tree and began looking for a suitable branch. The remaining two troopers tied Fred and Sam's hands tightly behind their backs, then took hold of Frisky and Spring's reins, and began leading them into position.

'Wait! Wait!' Fred called out suddenly. 'Hang on a minute, fellas. We're all men of the world here, we know what side our bread's buttered. Isn't there any kind of gift you would take in exchange for our lives?'

The trooper sergeant called for his men to halt. His eyes narrowed. A greedy smile played about his lips.

'Now you're talking, Mad Dog,' he said. 'You've got a stash somewhere, haven't you? A treasure trove, full of all the money and jewels you've stolen from banks over the years.'

'No,' Fred said. 'But I've got lots of cheese. How about a wagonload of my very best blue-veined Hairy-nose?'

'Kill him,' the trooper sergeant said. 'Hang him till his face turns blue and the crows peck out his eyes. His daughter too.'

'No!' Fred howled. 'What about *two* wagonloads? And some butter? And a side of wombat beef, freshly pickled?'

Stand in the shadow when shadows die, Sam repeated to herself. *What could it possibly mean?*

She and Fred were led into position, in the shade directly under the thickest branch of the tree.

'Excellent work, men!' the trooper sergeant said. 'Space them apart a bit . . . Good! That's it! Now hoist the ropes over the branch. That's the way! Lower the nooses over their heads . . . How does that rope feel against your neck, Mad Dog? Not hurting enough? Oh I'm so sorry, let me tighten it! Steady those kangaroos, boys, we don't want them bolting too early. Wait for the command. Don't do anything before I say.'

He dismounted and stood behind Fred and Sam. The nooses were now tight around their necks. The ropes looped up and over the branch, then down the other side. They were kept taut by two men standing a short distance away from the tree. All the trooper sergeant had to do now was slap Frisky and Spring hard enough to send them leaping forward, and Sam and Fred would be left swinging.

Sam felt a tear trickle slowly down her cheek. *I'm sorry it has to end like this, Billy,* she thought. *I promised to find a way to make you walk again. Now it'll never happen. Remember me in your dreams . . .*

The trooper sergeant took out a pocket watch. 'Noon!' he shouted. 'High noon! Hanging time!'

He raised both hands ready to slap the kangaroos. Sam looked up through the branches of the tree at the clear blue sky, one last time. She felt the warmth of the noonday sun even here, in the tree's shadow. She was about to close her eyes when . . .

Noon. She stiffened suddenly. *Noon is when shadows die, isn't it? Yes, it is! Not THIS shadow, because it's under a tree, but everywhere else, every other shadow fades away to nothing . . .*

She wasn't standing. She was sitting on roo-back. Did that matter?

'Dad, I think we're saved,' she said to Fred. 'I think it's all right, the Secret Door's going to open.'

She could almost feel it. There was a tingling and a crackling in the air, and a smell like the smell after lightning . . .

'*Die, you bushranging scum!*' the trooper sergeant shouted. '*HeeeYAAAAH!*'

He hit the two kangaroos on the behind as hard as he could. Spring leapt forward. Sam's saddle jerked from underneath her. She was falling. The noose was already tightening around her neck. She had just enough time to glance sideways and see that the same thing was happening to Fred.

Then she closed her eyes, and everything went white.

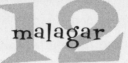

malagar

White.

Not black.

Sam knew she wasn't dead because she was still breathing. Somehow, the rope that had closed tight around her neck had disappeared.

She opened her eyes again. The whole world was white: above her, below her, all around. Everything else had vanished, except for her father, the trooper sergeant, and the two kangaroos. They were all frozen in mid-air underneath the tree. They were in exactly the same position they'd been in just before Sam closed her eyes. Her father was next to her, frozen in the act of falling to the ground. The two kangaroos were in front of her, frozen in the act of leaping away. And the trooper sergeant was behind her, frozen with his arms stretched low in front of him and his body leaning forward, like a swimmer about to dive into a pool.

A noise filled the air like a flash flood surging down a valley.

Colours began swirling in around Sam. Faster and faster they came, all the colours of the rainbow, mixing themselves into all manner of shapes before disappearing under more colours, and more shapes, in an ever-deepening spiral.

As quickly as it had begun, the whole thing stopped. The world wasn't white any more. A landscape had taken shape around Sam. It wasn't the landscape she had left a few moments earlier – the barren desert; the cracked red earth; the dead tree – but one completely different, and opposite in almost every way.

She was frozen above a patch of soft green grass, on the edge of a bubbling mountain stream. Beside her, so close that if she'd been able to move she could have touched them, were the broad, furry fronds of a large fern. A rainforest rose up all around. The sky was almost hidden by an overhanging canopy of leaves and vines and flowers. The stream in front of her cascaded over rocks and large, moss-covered stones into a deep pool, before continuing on through the forest.

Malagar! Sam thought, in a rush of delight. *We've made it! We're here at last!*

It was beautiful. It was just as she had imagined it in her dream. For a brief moment she worried that this *was* a dream, but then whatever spell was holding her in mid-air broke, and she fell tumbling to the grass.

She got up. Her father and the trooper sergeant had fallen not far away. The trooper sergeant had banged his head, and was lying on his stomach, groaning softly. Fred lay curled up tightly with his hands clasped over his eyes.

'I'm dead,' he gasped to himself. 'I *must* be dead. They hung me. But you know, for a dead person I don't feel so bad.'

'Dad!' Sam ran to him and threw her arms around his neck. 'It's me, Sam!'

Fred let out a wail of fear, and pushed her away. 'Begone, foul fiend!' he shouted. 'Get thee hence, Hound of Satan! Your evil magic won't fool me!'

'Dad, you're not dead,' Sam tugged at his arm. 'It's me. Open your eyes.'

Fred peered between two of his fingers. He blinked, and sat up.

'Is this Heaven or Hell?' he said. 'If it's Hell, these must be the good seats.'

'It's Malagar,' Sam said. 'The place I told you about, remember? With the Great Dingo?'

'The Great Dingo!' Fred's face lit up. 'So where is he? Is he here in the forest? Let me get my—— Drat.' He patted his holster. 'Those troopers took away my boomerangs.'

'And here they are, right here,' a familiar voice growled at them from further down the bank. 'I don't know where we are, or how we got here, Mad Dog. But you ruined my hanging and now you're going to pay.'

It was the trooper sergeant. His boomer-rifle had disappeared, but he was holding the two Colt .45s he'd confiscated from Fred and Sam. His eyes were sizzling with rage and his mouth was contorted into the most vicious-looking snarl that Sam had ever seen.

'Calm down, sergeant,' Fred said as he backed away. 'Don't shoot. I'll give you *three* wagonloads of cheese. And *two* sides of pickled wombat beef. And——'

Fred stopped, stunned. A dingo had stepped out from among the ferns and rushes on the far side of the stream. It stood upright on two legs, with its arms folded, grinning broadly. Sam knew at once that this was the same dingo she'd rescued from the waterhole back home – even if he *was* now wearing a loud Hawaiian shirt and mirror sunglasses, with a large white flower behind his ear.

'What's *that?*' the trooper sergeant yelped.

'That's a dingo,' Fred said. 'A dingo wearing a loud Hawaiian shirt and mirror sunglasses, with a large white flower behind its ear.'

'Why is it standing on two legs?' the trooper sergeant demanded. 'And what's it doing wearing clothes? I want some answers, Mad Dog, and I want them right now, or else I'll blow you away!'

'Ahem. I'm afraid I'll have to confiscate those boomerangs, sir,' the dingo said apologetically. 'Local council regulations. I'm sure you understand.'

At the sound of the dingo's voice, the trooper sergeant froze in horror. He turned and brandished the two boomerangs at the dingo threateningly.

'I don't know who or what you are,' he said. 'But you keep your filthy paws off me.'

The dingo sighed, and looked at Sam. 'An accident, huh?' he said. 'Has to be. I'm sure you wouldn't have brought him here on purpose.'

'He was trying to hang us,' Sam explained. 'He was standing under the tree when the Secret Door opened.'

'Three at once,' the dingo said thoughtfully.

'It's rare, but not unheard-of. Hasn't happened in about eleven thousand years.'

'So are you the *Great* Dingo?' Fred asked, in a suspicious voice. 'You don't look that great to me.'

'Me?' the dingo burst out laughing. 'Me, the Great Dingo? Are you kidding? I'm just the hired help. I'm strictly small potatoes, brother. The Great Dingo is as big as a mountain and as fierce as a thousand lions. When he speaks, the swiftest rivers stop flowing, and the tallest trees split asunder. His word is law.'

'Wow,' Fred said. He put his hand up to his mouth, and whispered to Sam, 'Maybe *four* pairs of slippers. And *two* rugs.'

'Enough!' the trooper sergeant interrupted. 'You with the shirt on, in the dingo suit! I'm a federal law enforcement officer in the middle of a hanging! I demand you give me back my ropes, my boomer-rifle, and my other five troopers!'

The dingo sighed a second time. He regarded the trooper sergeant sternly over the top of his sunglasses.

'Is he always like this?' he asked Sam.

'Right now he's in a *good* mood,' Sam said.

'I did ask him nicely,' the dingo went on. 'But I'll ask him again. Sir, you'll have to hand over those boomerangs. The Great Dingo is very sensitive about them, you know what I mean?'

'I'll hand 'em over all right,' the trooper sergeant growled 'I'll chop off your scrawny little pea-brained head with them, you –'

He raised his arm to throw, but never made it. At that exact same moment, the water in the pond in front of him exploded. Something enormous and horrible-looking came bursting up onto the bank. It was a crocodile – or at least that's what Sam thought at first. It had a crocodile's powerful jaws, short legs, and long, lizard-like body. But curling up behind it was a huge, deadly-looking scorpion's sting.

It grabbed the trooper sergeant in its jaws and hauled him back into the water. The trooper sergeant had just enough time to let out a short wail of terror before the surface of the pool closed over him and he was gone.

'There. *That's* better,' the dingo said, after a pause. He dusted his paws and peered down at the pool, to check that nothing was coming back up. Once the last ripple had settled he skipped across some stones further upstream, and trotted across the grass to Fred and Sam.

'So rude to threaten people when you're a tourist,' he said. 'Don't you think?'

'Wh-wh-wh –' Fred couldn't get the words out. 'What was *that?*' he managed to croak.

'That was a crocodorpion,' the dingo said. 'Or maybe a scorpocodile. It's *so* hard to tell them apart. There should be a couple more around. I'll call them for you, so you can have a closer look.'

'No! No!' Fred's cries of protest were drowned out by a sudden piercing whistle. Two innocent-looking logs floating at the far end of the pool came to life, and swam quickly towards them.

'Don't worry, they wouldn't hurt a fly,' the dingo said, as the two monstrous creatures hauled themselves onto the bank in front of Fred and Sam. 'Flies are insects, and these beauties don't eat insects. They eat juicy warm-blooded mammals, just like you.'

'Crikey,' Fred said. 'I don't know which end to run away from first.'

'The jaws of a crocodile, the tail of a scorpion,' Sam said. 'That's amazing. Are they native to Malagar?'

'They certainly are,' the dingo said proudly, stepping forward and patting one of the creatures on the back. 'And I'm glad you like them, because they're your transport. The only way to get to the Great Dingo is to go downstream, and these are faster than any boat or canoe. They won't eat you or sting you, as long as you ride them properly.'

'Did you say – *ride* them?' Fred said. 'No. You couldn't have. No one in their right mind would say that.'

'It's only a short trip,' the dingo went on cheerfully. 'Through the rapids and over the waterfall. Past the Marshes of the Dead and the Enchanted Mineral Springs and the Poisoned Ponds and the Bridge of Eternity. All the way into the Cave of Discovery, then down to the Sacred Pool of Miracles, the lair of the Great Dingo. He doesn't like to be kept waiting. We'd better go.'

kiss your mother goodbye

Sam glanced at her father. He was still staring at the crocodorpion in stunned disbelief, as though his worst nightmare had materialised right in front of him.

'If you think,' he said, 'if you think for *one second* that I'm getting on the back of that . . . that *thing* . . .'

'Does everyone who comes to Malagar travel like this?' Sam asked.

'All visitors do,' The dingo nodded. 'It's a highlight of the tour. Venice has gondolas. The Mississippi has steamboats. And we have man-eating crocodiles with stings. But listen, if you want to give up and turn back, that's fine. The Secret Door is always open. From *this* direction you can leave any time you like.'

'Great,' Fred said to Sam. 'Let's go. All we need is our—— Hey, wait a minute. What happened to our kangaroos?'

'They're being well looked after, don't worry,' the dingo said. 'Now, if you could just hop aboard your crocodorpion, sir. The Great Dingo doesn't like to be kept waiting.'

'You miserable little furball, you've eaten them, haven't you?' Fred stepped towards the dingo angrily, but retreated when both of the crocodorpions moved to block his path. 'All right,' he said. 'Maybe you haven't eaten them. Sorry I spoke.'

'Of course we haven't eaten them,' the dingo said patiently. 'They're our honoured guests. They've been put out to pasture in lush green fields, full of sweet juicy grass, tasty dandelions and beautiful girl kangaroos.'

'A likely story,' Fred grumbled. 'You can't pull the wombat fur over my eyes.'

Sam, meanwhile, had been studying the two crocodorpions very carefully. Without waiting for her father, she summoned her courage, and walked straight up to the nearest one. She swung a leg over its back, ducking as she did so to avoid its murderous sting, which was black and glistening, and the size of a large carving knife.

'See, Dad?' she said once she was seated. 'It's not going to hurt you. Get on.'

'Not on your nellie,' Fred said. 'I didn't escape from troopers and pythons and hangings and Taj Mahals to get munched by one of *those* things. Either we go the way civilised people go, on the back of a kangaroo, or we go home.'

With a sigh, the dingo put his paw up to his mouth, and let out a short, sharp whistle.

At once the crocodorpion next to Sam's sprang into action. It raced across the grassy bank at surprising speed, and grabbed Fred in its jaws. Fred let out a bellow of fear, and began bashing on the back of the crocodorpion's head with his fists, but the creature took no notice. With a casual flick of its neck it tossed Fred over its shoulder onto its back. Then it pinned him down with the flat end of its sting.

'Help, help!' Fred wailed. 'It's got me! It's stinging me to death! *Aaaah!*'

'You're a lucky man, Mr Tucker,' the dingo said. 'You get the safety harness. Mostly used by old women and very young children, but also, occasionally, by idiots. Now then. Everybody right to go?'

'I'm poisoned!' Fred howled. 'The venom is seeping into my veins!'

The dingo hopped up on the nose of the croc-odorpion that was carrying Sam, and adjusted its sunglasses. 'Just a few rules to announce before we leave,' he said. 'For your own safety, of course. No standing up during your journey. No eating or drink-ing. No jumping off the side. If you're wearing the safety harness, please keep your sting securely fastened. Oh, and before you go over the waterfall, don't forget to say a quick prayer and kiss your mother goodbye.'

'How high is it?' Sam asked.

'Not really *that* high,' the dingo said reassuringly. 'Only a thousand hops, straight down. Going over is perfectly safe. It's hitting the bottom that gets you, every time.'

Fred looked sick. He closed his eyes and groaned. At another whistle from the dingo, the two croco-dorpions turned and plunged into the water. Sam's led the way downstream, while Fred's followed close behind.

'Yeow! Crikey, it's freezing!' Fred bellowed, as the water closed up over his knees. 'That's it! I'm going to make slippers out of you, you mangy mongrel! And I'm going to wear them when I'm mucking out the milking shed! That's a promise!'

The dingo ignored him. 'So,' he said breezily to Sam, as he sat down cross-legged facing her on the tip of the crocodorpion's nose. 'Tell me how you got here. Did you have many adventures?'

'Just a few,' Sam said.

'But once you found the Sacred Tree, and figured out how to open the Secret Door, it was easy, right?'

'Not exactly,' Sam said. 'I didn't figure out how to open the door until the very last second. And it was the troopers who found the Sacred Tree, not us. If it wasn't for them, we'd still be wandering in the desert.'

'Oh.' The dingo looked thoughtful. 'So it was the *troopers* who found the tree. Maybe I shouldn't have killed that ugly fat one, then.'

'You had to,' Sam said. 'He was about to kill *you*.'

They rode on in silence. The crocodorpions were swimming at a cracking pace. Soon the stream they were travelling down joined up with another stream, and became wider.

'So what do you do here?' Sam asked the dingo. 'Are you the doorkeeper, or the gatekeeper, or something like that?'

'Close,' the dingo said. 'I'm the guide. I've been guiding all visitors to Malagar for fifteen thousand years.'

'You're *fifteen thousand years old*?' Sam said in astonishment. 'You're kidding!'

'I know, I know, I don't look a day over thirty,' the dingo said. 'I eat well, I work out, I don't drink too much, or lie in the sun. Of course I'm also immortal. That helps reduce the grey hairs.'

'Do many people come to Malagar?' Sam asked.

'No, not at all.' The dingo sighed. 'Hardly any. You see, nobody believes in legends any more. Or miracles, either, for that matter. The last person I took on this tour was a fierce Aboriginal warrior. That was three hundred and fifty years ago.'

Sam gaped at him. 'Are you saying,' she said, 'that we're the first people to come to Malagar in *three hundred and fifty years?*'

'Uh-huh.' The dingo nodded. 'So you can see why I'm excited. Things were getting a little slow.'

'And did he ... the warrior ... did he pass the Ultimate Test?' Sam asked, a little nervously.

'No.' The dingo shook his head. 'He failed.'

'What about the one before him?'

'That was a woman,' the dingo said. 'Five hundred years earlier. No, she didn't pass either.'

'What about the one before her?' Sam said, sounding more desperate now. 'Doesn't *anybody* pass this test?'

'Oh, sure.' The dingo nodded. 'We had one about five thousand years ago. A mighty chief who came to save his tribe from famine. He passed with flying colours.'

'He's the one in the story my mum used to tell me,' Sam said. 'But that's only one! You've only had *one person* pass the test, in all that time?'

'Of course not,' the dingo said. 'He was just the most recent. We've had a *lot* more than that in the fifteen thousand years I've been here. Two at least. Maybe three.'

Sam slumped forward despondently. 'I'll never do it!' she said. 'It's far too hard! I'm not a great warrior or a mighty chief! I'm just a wombat-farmer's daughter!'

'You don't even know what's *in* the test yet,' the dingo said.

'So what *is* in it?' Sam asked. 'What will I have to do?'

'Can't tell you.' The dingo grinned. 'Ha ha. Got your hopes up then, didn't I? All I can say is that you should think of the very hardest test you can imagine, and double it. That ought to get you close.'

Sam groaned. The icy waters of the stream were beginning to numb her feet and ankles, but she no longer cared.

Three people, in fifteen thousand years, she thought. *Who am I kidding? I'm going to fail miserably. I've come all this way for nothing.*

Meanwhile, not far behind her, her father had relaxed and was beginning to enjoy himself. He had rolled over onto his back and was stretched out lazily on his crocodorpion, with one hand tucked behind his head and the other trailing in the water.

'Y'know, Sam, these croco-scorpy things aren't so bad after all,' he said. 'I think we should take them home with us.' He plucked a handful of ripe purple berries from a branch overhanging the stream, and popped one of them into his mouth. 'They'd look great curled up on the front porch,' he went on. 'We could teach them to play "fetch" with travelling salesmen. And catch lots of troopers for them to eat.'

'Brace yourselves, folks!' the dingo interrupted. 'We're about to hit the rapids!'

Sure enough, around the very next bend, the stream narrowed and dropped steeply into a high-walled canyon. It tumbled between columns of boulders, each one the size of a house, then zig-zagged this way and that, slamming against the canyon walls with incredible force, shooting spray and foam high into the air.

'*Stop!*' Fred yelled. '*Stop the river! I want to get off!*'

White water engulfed them. Sam was terrified. Beneath her, the crocodorpion was straining, swerving and twisting with the raging torrent. The dingo, meanwhile, had got to his feet and was standing on the crocodorpion's nose with knees bent and arms out for balance, surfing for all he was worth.

'*Woo-hoo! Hang ten, baby!*' he shouted, as they shot around the first bend and immediately plunged into another. '*This is the only way to fly!*'

As quickly as they had come, the rapids were gone again. The river emerged from the canyon onto a broad, open plain. The two riverbanks were now a long way apart, allowing the sun to shine warmly down on the open water.

Sam sat quietly for a while, enjoying the feel of the sun on her soaking wet body. She didn't know if the weather was always like this in Malagar, but it certainly was a beautiful day. The dingo seemed to think so too. He had given up surfing, and was once more seated cross-legged on the crocodorpion's snout, scanning the river ahead of them, and humming happily to himself.

'Can I ask you a question?' Sam said.

'Sure.' The dingo turned to face her. 'Fire away.'

'What happens to the people who fail the Ultimate Test?' Sam said. 'The ones who don't get their miracle? Do you let them go again?'

'No,' the dingo said. 'Not exactly. You see, the Great Dingo is like a lot of gods – especially gods that live in caves, and don't see a lot of sun. He's kind of grumpy. If you fail, he demands that you be punished.'

'Punished?' Sam swallowed hard, trying to hide the fear in her voice. 'How? He doesn't *kill* people, surely.'

'No no, he'd never do that,' the dingo said. 'He might be grumpy, but he's not cruel. He simply makes them . . . change.'

'Into what?' Sam asked.

There was a long silence. Sam began to think the dingo wasn't going to answer. Then, so softly that she could hardly hear the words, he said, 'Into dingoes.'

Sam frowned. 'What d'you mean? Do you mean dingoes like you?'

'That's right. Exactly like me.'

Sam stared at him. All at once a whole lot of things made sense. She understood now how the dingo could talk. Why it lived in Malagar. And why it had tried to persuade her to come here, and try for a miracle herself.

'You were here!' she said breathlessly. 'Fifteen thousand years ago! You came like all those other people, to ask for a miracle!'

'Actually, no,' the dingo said ruefully. 'I came here by accident. Miracles were the last thing on my mind, believe me. I was standing under the Sacred Tree taking a leak, if you really want to know the truth. Then suddenly it was midday, I was right in the middle of the shadow, and – *bam!*'

'Oh no!' Sam burst out laughing. 'I don't believe it. That's hilarious.'

'Yessir, that's what I was doing all right.' The dingo sighed. 'Spraying the ol' fire hose. Taking a whizz. Cocking my leg against the trunk. Then next thing everything went white and I landed on a grassy bank next to a stream.'

'But who was there to meet you?' Sam said. 'Was it someone else's job to be the guide back then?'

'That's right,' the dingo said. 'Another dingo used to do it. He took me downstream to the Pool of Miracles, where I'm taking you now. And I met the Great Dingo. And I failed the Ultimate Test.'

'You failed?' Sam whispered.

'Miserably,' the dingo said. 'I was useless. I was a total washout. If they'd given me a score from one to a hundred, I would have got zero.'

The dingo lay down on his stomach, resting his jaw on his paws. 'But hey, that's life,' he said philosophically. 'These things happen. One day you're a human. The next day you're a dog.'

'Don't you miss being human?' Sam asked.

'I can't even remember what it was like.' The dingo shrugged. 'Fifteen thousand years is a very long time. After ten thousand years you get set free, you know. The Great Dingo turns you loose again, and gives you the choice to stay or go. So I could go back to being a human any time I like.'

'Why don't you?' Sam asked.

'Because I'm a dingo now,' the dingo grinned. 'I'm a *Malagar* dingo, that walks on two legs, and talks. I've got a great job. I get to travel. I get to wear these cool sunglasses and this classy Hawaiian shirt. And you know the part I like best of all?'

'No, what?'

'I get to help other people try for a miracle. Like you.'

The dingo sat up again, and stretched. He cast a casual glance at the sports watch his wrist, then leapt to his feet.

'Holy smoke!' he yelped. 'We're late! We're *way* behind schedule! We need to seriously switch on the turbos!'

Before Sam could ask what was happening he let out three short, urgent whistles. The crocodorpions seemed to know exactly what this signal meant. They lowered their heads, swished their tails, and began swimming as if their lives depended on it.

Sam felt a surge underneath her. The water around her legs began to bubble and boil. Somehow her crocodorpion managed to lift itself up, almost out of the water, and began skimming along the surface. A great frothing, foaming wave rose up behind it, like a breaker rolling towards a beach.

Faster and faster the crocodorpion skimmed. The wind rushed through Sam's hair. She turned to see that Fred's crocodorpion was swimming just as quickly.

'This is incredible!' she shouted to the dingo. 'How can they go this fast?'

'Jet propulsion,' the dingo replied. 'If you look at their mouths, you'll see they've got their jaws wide open under the water. See that? They're sucking water in, gallons and gallons of it every second, then squirting it out their backsides just as quickly. But they can go a whole lot faster than this.'

He gave another, even louder, whistle. Sam's crocodorpion lifted itself up still higher. It began planing down the middle of the river at a simply unbelievable speed. It was now going so fast it could barely steer itself around corners.

'That's the ticket! Now we're cooking with gas!' The dingo stood up and spread his arms wide. 'Feel the wind in your hair! Taste the spray in your mouth! Then say a prayer and kiss your mother goodbye, because we're about to go over the waterfall! A thousand hops straight down, into a churning maelstrom of thundering white water and jagged rocks! Over we *go-o-o-o!*'

Travelling side by side, the two crocodorpions shot around one more bend in the river and over the top of the waterfall. The land and the river fell away giddyingly underneath them. All at once, Sam could see forest spreading out in every direction, over high, rolling hills and sweeping plains. The river that had seemed so wide and deep a few moments earlier was now nothing more than a tiny silvery trail.

'Mummy!' Fred hollered, throwing his arms around his crocodorpion's neck and hugging it as if it really was his mother. *'We're going down! I can't hold her! Houston, this is Wombat Farmer One, do you read me? She's breaking up!'*

To Sam's astonishment, the two crocodorpions did *not* go down. They had launched themselves off the top of the waterfall at such speed, with such great forward momentum, that they continued to fly straight through the air. They did begin falling eventually, but it was a very gradual and pleasant descent, almost like a glider coming into land.

Fred, however, was still panicking. *'She's breaking up!'* he yelled again. *'Mayday! Wombat Farmer One to Base! Do you copy?'*

'Calm yourself, Mr Tucker!' the dingo called to

him. 'Everything's perfectly under control! We'll be landing in just a few minutes, not far from the entrance to the Cave of Discovery. We will then taxi a short distance through the cave to the Sacred Pool of Miracles, for your audience with the Great Dingo. And in case you're wondering what happened to the other highlights that were promised on the tour, let me inform you that the route we've taken today is the Express Route. It skips the Marshes of the Dead, and the Enchanted Mineral Springs, and the Poisoned Ponds, and the Bridge of Eternity – which is just as well, really. They're all boring as bat-farts. And now, as we come in sight of our final destination, let me thank you on behalf of the crocodorpions and crew. It's been a pleasure having you aboard.'

facing the great dingo

A short time later the two crocodorpions came swooping down to land. The landing was not without a few bumps and splashes – especially when Sam's crocodorpion just missed crashing into a tree – but compared to shooting off the top of a waterfall, both Sam and Fred found it quite tame.

'Here we are,' the dingo said cheerfully, once the crocodorpions had recovered, and were swimming normally again. 'Right outside the Cave of Discovery. And right on time.'

They had entered a steep, rocky valley hung with grasses and palm trees and ferns. Flocks of brightly coloured parrots screeched from the treetops. Once again, because of the hills on either side of the river, the surface of the water was in shadow. The scene before them was bathed in an eerie, ghostly radiance, as if lit up at midnight by a full moon.

They were about to enter a magnificent underground cave.

The entrance to this cave was quite low. It arched smoothly overhead like the opening of a tunnel. As they passed inside, Sam could see thousands of tiny, brilliant glow-worms shining from the walls. Further in, the tunnel opened out to form an enormous cavern with a high, domed ceiling. At the base of this cavern the river widened into a mirror-smooth underground lake.

'Is this the Pool of Miracles?' she asked the dingo.

'Not yet,' the dingo replied. 'It's still the Cave of Discovery. We need to go a bit further in.'

'Why is it called the Cave of Discovery?' Sam asked.

'Because it marks the spot where the Great Dingo found his first bone, many millions of years ago,' the dingo said. 'Legend has it that the Great Dingo came here from Sirius, the Dog Star. The whole of Malagar was completely flat back then. The Great Dingo began digging everywhere, looking for bones, and as he dug he created the hills and mountains that you see today. He dug for a million years without finding a single bone, so you can imagine he was getting pretty hungry. When he finally *did* find a bone, he cried for joy. And those tears became the Sacred Pool of Miracles, the holiest site in all of Malagar.'

'Is he really as big as a mountain and as fierce as a thousand lions?' Sam asked anxiously.

'You bet,' the dingo said.

'And he'll change me into a dingo if I fail the Ultimate Test?'

'Absolutely. If he doesn't incinerate you with a bolt of flaming dog-breath first. But he'll only do that if you're rude.'

'That's what I like about you, Dingo,' Sam said. 'You really know how to cheer a girl up.' She paused for a moment, then went on, 'I wish you'd tell me more about the Ultimate Test. I get the shivers just thinking about it. I'm going to be too scared to do anything, I know it.'

'Being scared's all right,' the dingo said. 'It keeps you on your toes. If you *weren't* scared, that would be a worry.'

'Will I have to fight dragons?' Sam said. 'Or ward off evil spirits? Or walk through pits of fire?'

'No. Nothing like that.'

'No monsters to fight? No horrible ordeals?'

The dingo shook his head. 'Nope.'

'So what is it, then? You said to think of the hardest test I could think of, and double it.' Sam was seized with a sudden suspicion. 'It's not maths, is it? I bet it is. I'm hopeless at maths. Unless it's counting wombats, I'm okay at that.'

'It's not maths,' the dingo said.

'What about spelling?' Sam went on. 'I can spell stroganoff. Listen: S-T-R-O——'

'No spelling either.'

'No monsters, no ordeals, no maths, no spelling?' Sam frowned in puzzlement. 'What *is* it? You could at least give me a clue, Dingo. You owe me. I'm the one who rescued you, remember?'

'No clues,' the dingo said firmly. 'I gave you the clue to find the Secret Door, but when you take the Ultimate Test, you take it alone.'

A short time later they came to the far shore of the lake. Although they were now deep underground, and the entrance behind them had long since disappeared, the walls of the cavern were still covered in glow-worms. They could see the way ahead quite clearly.

Sam made out a wide, smooth shelf of rock, stretching away beyond the edge of the cavern into darkness. In the middle of this shelf was the Sacred Pool. It was the size of a large duckpond, and gave off a faint, sparkling white light, very different from the milky yellow light cast by the glow-worms.

'That's the lair of the Great Dingo,' the dingo whispered, pointing beyond the Sacred Pool into the inky darkness which hung like a giant curtain before them. 'He dwells there in stillness and silence, through the long ages, and reveals himself only when the waters of the pool are disturbed by a visitor. When that happens, a mighty stone at the top of the cavern rolls away, light shines down upon the pool from high above, and the Great Dingo comes forth. Then all the dingoes of Malagar gathers together, and the Test is given, and there is great feasting and celebration. Unless the visitor fails, of course. That's usually a bit of a bummer.'

The two crocodorpions reached the lake's edge. The dingo leapt off nimbly, and led the way up the gently sloping rock. Sam and Fred followed. Fred kept glancing around nervously, as if expecting to get attacked by something extremely nasty at any second. He stumbled and almost fell.

'Mr Tucker.' The dingo turned to him with a toothy grin. 'So glad to see you've arrived safe and well. Was there anything we could have done to make your trip more comfortable?'

Fred thought for a second. 'Some popcorn would

have been nice,' he said. 'And maybe an in-flight movie.'

'Now that you're here, at the Sacred Pool of Miracles, I need to ask you a question,' the dingo went on. 'Do you intend to take the Ultimate Test along with your daughter?'

'Me?' Fred blinked. 'Take the Ultimate Test? Sure, why not? I'm pretty good at stuff like that.'

'When was the last time you took a test, Mr Tucker?' the dingo asked.

'Hmm. Let me see now.' Fred rubbed his chin. 'When I was three years old. The doctor asked me to walk in a straight line, and sing "Happy Birthday". I did it, too. Only not both at the same time.'

'This test is just a *little* bit different,' the dingo said. 'If you pass, you get a miracle. If you fail, you get turned into a dingo. Only three people have passed in the last fifteen thousand years.'

'Only three people in . . .' Fred's voice trailed away. He reached down quickly and shook the dingo's paw. 'Thanks,' he said. 'Thanks *so* much. Nice of you to offer, but I'm out of training right now. This is my off-season for Ultimate Tests. I'll just coach from the sidelines.'

'I'm afraid you can't do that,' the dingo said. 'Those who take the test must do so alone and unaided. You'll have to stay here at the water's edge, and remain completely silent.'

'Okay,' Fred said. 'What about if I cheer? You know, something catchy and original, like: 'Give me an S! Give me an A! Give me an M! What does it spell? GO, TEAM!'

'*Completely* silent.' The dingo said firmly. 'Not even a whistle.' Glancing at Sam, he added, 'Come on. It's time to go.'

Sam set off with the dingo across the rock shelf. She had never felt more lonely or frightened in her life. She was on her own now. There could be no turning back. No changing her mind. No excuses. Soon it would be just her and the Great Dingo, and the test would begin.

She knew exactly what she would ask for, if she was granted her miracle. She would ask simply for Billy to be healed. More than anything else she wanted Billy to be fit and healthy again, so he could ride with her up on Sunstroke Ridge, and help his family run the wombat farm, the way he used to.

'Here it is, Sam,' the dingo said. He paused at the edge of the Sacred Pool, and placed a paw lightly on her arm. 'Kneel down and touch the water with your fingertips. The rest will follow.'

Sam knelt down. As she went to touch the water

with her hand, she gave a tiny gasp. There, staring back at her from the surface, was a perfect reflection of herself – an exact double, down to the finest detail.

The reflection moved, like an image on a screen. It became a picture of her combing her hair in her bedroom. Then it changed to become a picture of her in dirty overalls, outside the milking shed. Next it became a picture of her wearing her very best dress – the dress she had last worn on Billy's birthday, several months earlier, when the family had celebrated in Billy's bedroom.

This last picture faded. Another came into view. This was a picture of Sam's father, her mother, and Billy, also dressed in the clothes they had worn for Billy's birthday. They were standing on the front porch. Behind them was the family homestead. Smoke was rising from its chimney.

One after another, all sorts of pictures from Sam's life appeared and faded. Frisky and Spring in the stables. The view from Sunstroke Ridge. The wombat herd grazing under the gum trees. Sam saw herself rescuing the dingo from the dried-up waterhole. Then she was in the bank at Backward Point, with her father, pointing a boomerang at the bank clerk. Another picture showed her escaping from Deepfry Canyon up the path that Billy had found. Yet another showed the trooper sergeant smiling cruelly as he placed a noose around her father's neck.

It's my memory, Sam thought. *The pool is showing me my own memory. It can see into my mind.*

She reached down and touched the cool water with the tips of her fingers. At once her reflection, and the pictures behind it, disappeared. The surface of the pool began to sparkle and dance in front of her, so brightly that she had to shield her eyes.

There was a noise behind her. She turned to see that a large crowd of dingoes was gathering at the far end of the cavern. Several hundred of them were now standing on the rock shelf, a short distance from her, at the base of the cavern wall. A few stragglers were still coming out of holes in the wall behind, pushing and shoving as they moved forward, trying to get a view.

From a long way overhead, in the darkness at the very top of the cavern, there came a low, scraping noise. Sam saw a crack of light appearing. It grew wider. The scraping continued until the crack had become a perfect circle. By this time, enough light was shining down to illuminate the entire cavern.

It lit up the walls, and the dingoes, and the lake, and the rock shelf, and the Sacred Pool. It also lit up the thick inky blackness *beyond* the Sacred Pool, so that for the first time Sam could see into the Great Dingo's lair.

The Great Dingo was sitting in the corner. He was watching her intently, with his tail curled around his front paws. He had been watching her all the time.

He was not quite as big as a mountain, although he seemed almost that big to Sam. He was as tall as the cavern itself. His eyes were a deep, glowing red, and there was something strange about his fur. It didn't seem quite the right colour. It was darker than normal, and strangely smooth, and hard-looking, as if it was made of——'

'Sam! Hey, Sam! Is that dingo huge or what?'

Sam spun around. Her father was behind her, pointing at the Great Dingo and grinning.

'Think of the slippers, Sam!' he said excitedly. 'Think of the *rugs*! We could have wall-to-wall dingo-skin carpet! Dingo-skin tablecloths! Dingo-skin towels! Dingo-skin curtains and——'

'Dad, you're not supposed to be here!' Sam hissed. 'Get back! You'll ruin everything!'

'WHO DARES TALK OUT OF TURN IN THE PRESENCE OF THE GREAT DINGO?'

The voice that rang out was so deep and powerful that it made the walls of the cavern shake. A pile of loose rocks came tumbling down from high above the rock shelf, narrowly missing the audience of watching dingoes.

'Now you're for it!' one of the dingoes called out to Fred.

'It's the dog-breath for you, mate!' another one called.

All at once there was a great stamping and clapping of paws, and all the dingoes began chanting, '*Dog-breath! Dog-breath! Dog-breath!*'

'SILENCE!' the Great Dingo growled. 'I MUST BE ANSWERED! WHO IS IT THAT APPROACHES THE POOL OF MIRACLES UNHERALDED, AND DARES TALK OUT OF TURN?'

Fred stood up as straight as he could. 'I'm sorry, Your Muttfulness,' he said. 'That would be my daughter Sam. We've tried to bring her up right, to be seen and not heard, but sometimes she just shoots her mouth off without thinking, and——'

'YOU!' the Great Dingo snarled, his eyes glowing redder than hot coals. 'YOU ARE THE ONE OF WHOM I SPEAK! YOU DARE TALK ABOUT TURNING ME INTO A TABLECLOTH?'

There was a loud '*Ooooooo!*' from the watching dingoes. 'Start grovelling, buddy!' one of them called. 'You're about to be frizzled!'

Fred got down on his knees, and clasped his

hands in front of him. 'Your Dogginess,' he pleaded. 'Your Houndfulness. Your Poochiness. I'm only a humble wombat farmer. I——'

'He didn't mean it, O Great One,' Sam interrupted, stepping forward. 'It was just a joke. He knows he could never turn you into a tablecloth, or any of those other things he mentioned, for he sees very clearly that you are made of stone.'

'I do?' Fred said. 'I mean . . . I do! That's right! You're made of stone, Your Muttfulness! Any idiot could see that! Not much call for stone tablecloths, where I come from.'

'VERY WELL,' the Great Dingo said, after a pause. 'YOUR DAUGHTER HAS SAVED YOU. YOU MAY RETIRE.'

'Retire?' Fred said. 'But I'm only thirty-nine!'

'He means go back!' Sam hissed. 'Go back to the edge of the lake! Hurry!'

Fred got to his feet and hurried back across the rock shelf. 'Made of stone. Sheesh,' he muttered to himself. 'No use to me at all. Although he'd look all right next to the fishpond, in the back yard . . .'

'AND NOW, SAMANTHA TUCKER,' the Great Dingo said, 'YOUR TIME HAS COME. STEP FORWARD, IF YOU ARE READY, AND TAKE THE ULTIMATE TEST.'

the ultimate test

15

'You know my name?' Sam said.

'OF COURSE. I KNOW EVERYTHING ABOUT YOU,' the Great Dingo said, 'FOR THE SACRED POOL HAS REVEALED YOUR MEMORY TO ME. I KNOW YOUR HEART'S DEEPEST DESIRES.'

'Do you know what miracle I'm going to ask for?' Sam said.

'YES,' the Great Dingo said. 'BUT WHAT YOU *INTEND* TO ASK FOR, AND WHAT YOU *ACTUALLY* ASK FOR, CAN BE TWO DIFFERENT THINGS. PEOPLE HAVE BEEN KNOWN TO CHANGE THEIR MINDS.'

'I won't change mine,' Sam said.

'THAT REMAINS TO BE SEEN,' the Great

Dingo said. 'ARE YOU READY TO TAKE THE ULTIMATE TEST?'

'Yes,' Sam said.

She was standing as close as she dared to the feet of the Great Dingo, looking up into its glowing red eyes. She glanced quickly behind her, searching for the dingo guide, but he had disappeared. *He must have taken his place with the rest of the dingoes*, she thought. *I'm sure he'll be watching, and cheering me on.*

'I SEE THAT YOU AND YOUR FAMILY HAVE SUFFERED MUCH,' the Great Dingo said. 'I ALSO SEE THAT THIS PAINS YOU, FOR YOU LOVE YOUR FAMILY DEARLY. YOU HAVE JOURNEYED FAR, AND OVERCOME MANY PERILS, ON THEIR BEHALF.'

'Yes, O Great One,' Sam said. 'I love my family more than anything in the world.'

'I DO NOT DOUBT IT,' the Great Dingo said. 'AND NOW, SAMANTHA TUCKER, YOUR TEST BEGINS. FIRST, TELL ME EXACTLY WHO YOUR MIRACLE IS FOR.'

That was easy. 'It's for my brother Billy,' Sam said, taking a deep breath and forcing herself to speak more clearly. 'He was crippled in a riding accident. I want him to be well again.'

There was a long silence. Not a murmer came

from the crowd of watching dingoes. Sam could feel her heart thumping in her chest. Her knees were trembling. The palms of both her hands were clammy with sweat.

'YOU DO NOT DESIRE ANYTHING FOR YOURSELF?' The Great Dingo enquired. 'GREAT RICHES? GREAT BEAUTY? GREAT TALENT?'

Sam hesitated. Of course there were many things she wanted for herself. She had never seen the ocean, for example. She had never owned a new dress. She had never been to the city, or attended a concert, or eaten a meal that didn't have wombat in it. There were so many, many things . . .

'No,' she said, and swallowed hard. 'Nothing is as important as making Billy well again.'

'VERY WELL,' the Great Dingo said. 'YOU HAVE PASSED THE FIRST PART OF THE TEST. A MIRACLE IS A GIFT OF LOVE. IT CAN NEVER BE GRANTED TO THE PERSON WHO ASKS FOR IT. IF YOU HAD ASKED FOR SOME-THING FOR YOURSELF, I WOULD HAVE BEEN FORCED TO STRIKE YOU DOWN WITH A BOLT OF FLAMING DOG-BREATH. AND THAT WOULD NOT HAVE BEEN PRETTY.'

'Oh,' Sam said, feeling both legs go as wobbly as jelly. 'No, it wouldn't.'

'THE SECOND AND FINAL PART OF THE TEST IS ALSO A QUESTION,' the Great Dingo went on. 'IT IS AT ONCE INFINITELY SIMPLE, AND INFINITELY COMPLEX. YOU MAY ANSWER ONLY WITH A YES OR A NO.'

Sam waited. Her heart was now pounding so hard that her ribs were juddering. She had imagined the Ultimate Test to be many things – monsters, ghosts, pits of fire – but not this. Everything now depended on a simple yes or no.

'ARE YOU, SAMANTHA, PREPARED TO DIE FOR YOUR MIRACLE?' the Great Dingo asked.

Sam swallowed. She felt dizzy. She staggered as her legs momentarily gave way. *So that's it*, she thought to herself. *That's how you get your miracle. You have to die before it's granted.*

A gift of love, the Great Dingo had said. Her life for Billy's. It was obvious now. She really should have thought of it earlier.

Could she say yes? Could she sacrifice herself so that Billy would be healed? A part of her protested loudly. She was only twelve years old. There were so many things she hadn't done. But the farm and her family were the important things in her life. Every-thing else was an extra, a luxury . . .

She wanted to look around at her father, and try and find the dingo guide, but she couldn't. They wouldn't be any help to her now, anyway. She had to make the decision on her own.

Am I prepared to die to heal Billy and save the farm? she thought. *Am I? Am I?*

'Yes,' she said out loud to the Great Dingo. She repeated the word, still louder. 'Yes, yes.'

A great cheer rose up from the watching dingoes. They threw their paws in the air and hooted and howled and danced around. At first Sam didn't understand why they were celebrating. She had been forced to offer up her life, which was a terrible thing. But it was also a *heroic* thing, and perhaps it was her heroism that the dingoes were celebrating.

As Sam stood gazing up at the Great Dingo through blurred, watery eyes, she heard another sound. A sound so loud it almost drowned out the cheering.

It was the sound of a man shouting at the top of his lungs.

'No-o-o-o-o-o!'

Sam turned to see Fred running full pelt towards her. Before she could move, he swept her up into his arms and set off with her, back across the rock shelf. The watching dingoes ceased their cheering, and ran to surround them. A few seconds later every escape route was blocked off. Slowly and menacingly, the dingoes closed in.

'Put her down, clown,' one of them said.

'Let her go, Joe,' another one said.

'Now you're *really* for it,' another said. 'It's the dog-breath for you, for sure.'

Still carrying Sam in his arms, Fred turned to face the Great Dingo defiantly.

'You can't do this!' he burst out. '*She* can't do this! She's only twelve years old!'

'BE SILENT, MR TUCKER,' the Great Dingo said. 'THIS IS YOUR LAST WARNING. YOU HAVE NO BUSINESS HERE.'

'Yes I do! She's my daughter!' Fred bellowed. 'She's everything to me! You can't kill her!'

'SHE HAS PASSED THE ULTIMATE TEST,' the Great Dingo said. 'SHE HAS CHOSEN TO DIE FOR HER MIRACLE. NO MAN MAY SET THIS CHOICE ASIDE.'

'Then take me instead!' Fred said. 'Please! Let me die instead of her!'

'No, Dad, no!' Sam wriggled free of her father's arms, and stood in front of him. 'This whole thing was my idea! I'm responsible, not you! It *has* to be me! And besides, Mum and Billy need you way too much!'

'They need you too, Sammy,' Fred said. 'More than you'll ever know.'

'You can't do it!' Sam insisted. 'And that's final!'

'Hey!' Fred glared at her crossly. 'I'm the expert bushranger, remember? And you're just the raw recruit! If I say it's me, then it's *me*, okay?'

'SILENCE!' the Great Dingo commanded. 'IF THERE'S ONE THING I CAN'T STAND, IT'S PETTY DOMESTIC SQUABBLES!'

Total silence descended.

'FREDERICK TUCKER,' the Great Dingo continued. 'YOU HAVE PASSED THROUGH THE SECRET DOOR. YOU HAVE JOURNEYED TO THE SACRED POOL. IT IS YOUR RIGHT TO TAKE THE ULTIMATE TEST IF YOU DESIRE TO DO SO.'

'You bet your stone slippers I do!' Fred said. 'My miracle is the same as Sam's and yes, I *am* ready to die for it! So put *that* in your tablecloth and smoke it!'

'SO BE IT,' the Great Dingo said. 'IT IS DECIDED. YOU SHALL DESCEND INTO THE WATERS OF THE SACRED POOL IN PLACE OF YOUR DAUGHTER.'

A second great cheer rose up from the dingoes. A short distance away, the surface of the Sacred Pool began to sparkle and glitter. Fred stared at the pool grimly. He hardly noticed when Sam began tugging at his arm.

'It shouldn't be you, it should be me!' Sam said. 'You can't do this! I won't let you do this!'

Fred crouched down beside her. 'Listen, Sam,' he said. 'I'm nearly forty years old. I've lived much longer than you. I've fallen in love. I've got married. I've built a house. I've owned a farm, and I've had two beautiful kids. You should have the chance to do these things too, if you want to. Or travel, or go adventuring, whatever you like. I know I'm not the smartest man in the world. I've done some stupid things. I've let you down. But I'm going to die instead of you, Sam. And nothing you can do or say is going to stop me.'

Sam couldn't speak. For once all she wanted was to be wrapped up in one of her father's spine-crushing hugs, and feel like a freshly squeezed orange.

They hugged for the last time. Sam stepped aside. A strange calmness had settled over her. She felt as if she was floating on air.

She was ready to let her father die.

the miracle of malagar

16

'STEP FORWARD, FREDERICK TUCKER,' the Great Dingo said. 'YOU MAY APPROACH THE SACRED POOL.'

'Okay, Sam, this is it,' Fred said. 'After I'm gone, you can have all my slippers. And my rugs. And my wombat milking bucket. And remember, if you want to rob a bank you need a *very* big kangaroo.'

'I'll miss you, Dad,' Sam said.

'Don't be sad,' Fred replied. 'Think about Billy. You and he will run the farm much better than I did.'

He went to go, but turned back one final time. 'You can finish my ballad for me too,' he said. 'I never did find anything to rhyme with "python".'

With that he began walking towards the pool. The dingoes that were blocking his path quickly moved out of his way. When he reached the water's edge he paused and looked up at the Great Dingo.

'What do I do now?' he said.

'WALK OUT UPON THE WATER,' the Great Dingo said.

'Okay.' Fred shrugged. 'If you say so. Here goes nothing.'

He stepped out onto the sparkling surface of the pool. He didn't sink. He took another step, and found that he could walk on the surface of the water, exactly as if it were glass.

'WALK RIGHT OUT TO THE MIDDLE,' the Great Dingo instructed him.

Fred took another step. And another. When he reached the middle he stopped and waited.

'IT IS TIME TO SAY FAREWELL, FREDERICK TUCKER,' the Great Dingo said. 'YOUR MIRACLE SHALL BE GRANTED. YOUR SON SHALL BE HEALED. IN MALAGAR YOU WILL FOREVER BE COUNTED AMONG THE BRAVEST AND NOBLEST OF HEROES. IF YOU ARE STILL READY TO DIE, CLOSE YOUR EYES.'

Sam held her breath.

Fred closed his eyes.

With a bubbling and a frothing, the waters of the Sacred Pool began closing around his ankles. They closed up over his knees and thighs. They closed up just as quickly over his waist and his chest. Sam couldn't watch. She pressed both hands to her face, then peered out from between her fingers.

The water was closing over Fred's mouth. Over his eyes, his forehead, and his hair . . .

'Dad!' she cried out, at the top of her voice. 'Dad, I love you!'

Then he was gone. Sam fell to the ground, and everything went white.

White.

Not black.

A rumbling noise filled the air. It was the noise of a flash flood surging down a valley. Colours began rushing in. All the shades of the rainbow came pouring in around her, mixing themselves into brilliant and beautiful shapes, swirling in an ever-deepening spiral.

Then it stopped.

Sam found herself back home.

She was frozen in mid-air above the path leading to the homestead. It was late afternoon, heading towards evening. To her right was the milking shed. The herd of wombats was gathered patiently in the paddock beside it, waiting to be milked.

Just up ahead was the stables. There, tethered to

a post, were Frisky and Spring, taking a long, cool drink from their trough.

A wisp of grey smoke was curling up from the chimney at the homestead. The smell of wombat stroganoff wafted down on the breeze.

The dingo guide was standing on the path just in front of her. He was still dressed in the same shirt and sunglasses, with the same large white flower behind his ear.

Sam dropped to the ground. She got up at once, and dusted herself off.

'You!' she said. 'How did you get here? No, never mind that. Did the miracle work? Is Billy healed?'

The dingo did not speak. He merely gestured up the path with his paw, towards the homestead.

Sam blinked. *No,* she thought. *I must be seeing things. That can't be real.*

Her father was standing on the front porch. Next to him was her mother. They were both grinning and waving frantically, welcoming her home.

'But that's impossible!' she blurted out to the dingo. 'My father's dead! He gave his life, so that Billy could be healed!'

'The Great Dingo asked only that he be *ready* to die,' the dingo replied. 'It was a test of his love for your brother. You both passed the test, Sam. Only the fourth time it's been done in fifteen thousand years.'

As soon as the dingo had finished these words, he disappeared. Sam found herself staring at nothing but an empty space on the path. There was no time to wonder what had happened, for she could hear voices now: joyful, exhilarated voices floating down the hill. Her mother and father were calling to her from the homestead. And someone else was calling as well.

'Sam! Sam, look! I can walk again! I'm healed!'

She looked up. The front door of the homestead had been flung open. There on the porch, standing between her mother and her father, was Billy.

He gave a shout of laughter and started to run.